BARBARIAN

STRICTLY
TABOO

STRICTLY TABOO

JAID BLACK

BERKLEY SENSATION, NEW YORK

THE BERKLEY PUBLISHING GROUP
Published by the Penguin Group
Penguin Group (USA) Inc.
375 Hudson Street, New York, New York 10014, USA
Penguin Group (Canada), 90 Eglinton Avenue East, Suite 700, Toronto, Ontario M4P 2Y3, Canada
(a division of Pearson Penguin Canada Inc.)
Penguin Books Ltd., 80 Strand, London WC2R 0RL, England
Penguin Group Ireland, 25 St. Stephen's Green, Dublin 2, Ireland (a division of Penguin Books Ltd.)
Penguin Group (Australia), 250 Camberwell Road, Camberwell, Victoria 3124, Australia
(a division of Pearson Australia Group Pty. Ltd.)
Penguin Books India Pvt. Ltd., 11 Community Centre, Panchsheel Park, New Delhi—110 017, India
Penguin Group (NZ), Cnr. Airborne and Rosedale Roads, Albany, Auckland 1310, New Zealand
(a division of Pearson New Zealand Ltd.)
Penguin Books (South Africa) (Pty.) Ltd., 24 Sturdee Avenue, Rosebank, Johannesburg 2196,
South Africa

Penguin Books Ltd., Registered Offices: 80 Strand, London WC2R 0RL, England

STRICTLY TABOO

This book is an original publication of The Berkley Publishing Group.

First edition: December 2005

Berkley Sensation trade paperback ISBN: 0-425-20245-3

This book has been catalogued with the Library of Congress.

PRINTED IN THE UNITED STATES OF AMERICA

10   9   8   7   6   5   4   3   2   1

CONTENTS

BARBARIAN

1

NEMESIS

111

NAUGHTY NANCY

A Trek Mi Q'an Tale

191

Chapter 1

January 7, 878 A.D.
Chippenham, Wessex

"Nay," she murmured. Color rapidly drained from her cheeks as she watched the grisly sight unfold. Her breathing grew labored and her heart dropped into her stomach as she saw one of her sire's men fall to the ground, decapitated by a Viking's sword. She felt nigh close to fainting. "Nay," she whispered again, pulling the heavy cloak tightly around her.

Lady Elen of Godeuart was too shocked and horrified to say aught more. Never had she thought to see her family's mighty stronghold fall to the heathen Northmen, yet it was precisely what was happening.

"Bloody infidels!" Lothar of Godeuart swore. His nostrils flared as he stood upon the parapet with Elen watching the mayhem below unfold. "The king should have known the savages would break their word!"

Elen turned her worried gaze to her eldest brother. She fought with the ferocious icy-cold wind to keep her long blonde curls from lashing into her face. "I—I thought King Alfred paid the Northmen much Danegeld to leave Wessex and return to Mercia." Her lips were parched, her throat dry. "Lothar, I'm afraid." She breathed. "What do we—"

"Stay here, Elen," he cut in, reaching for his sword. "I shall return for you the soonest. Do as I say and keep yourself from harm's way."

"Lothar—nay!" Panic engulfed her at the thought of her brother confronting the Viking marauders. Her heart pounded against her chest as she reached for his tunic sleeve and pulled. "I beseech you not to go down there! Already Father is lost to us. I could not bear it were you to—"

"Elen," Lothar said with gentle insistence, "I must go." Her eldest brother was an unsmiling, stoic man, mayhap, yet Elen could see his love for her there in his eyes. "I will return to you. I swear it."

She nodded, her breasts heaving up and down in time with her labored breathing. "May God be with you and mighty Wessex." Her apprehensive gaze followed Lothar until he was well out of sight.

Elen's attention returned to the carnage below. When first she had heard tell that the savages had stormed Chippenham last eve, she had known deep within herself that the Godeuart holding would be one of the first attacked. Verily, the keep was built entirely of stone, a rarity in the region and one that underlined the wealth of her family.

She had known the Vikings would attack her ancestral holding, yet Elen had never truly believed her beloved home would fall.

It *was* falling. Rapidly. And, what's more, there was only but a handful of King Alfred's men left to defend it.

Never in all of her nineteen years had Elen witnessed a slaughter the likes of which she was seeing this morn. Her brother, Lothar, had mayhap been overprotective of her since Papa's death, but then Elen was one of only four Godeuart progeny—and the only daughter—to have survived past childhood.

Sweet Beatrix had died of fever at the age of two. Gisela had died at birth along with their mother. Verily, out of the nine children Lady Helene had carried in her womb, only Elen and three of her brothers had endured. Such was the reality of their world.

After the death of their father, Asser, in a bloody battle with the Vikings a year past, Lothar had been all the more determined to marry his sister off to a warlord with vast holdings who was in favor with the king. He wanted Elen's protection from a man capable of giving it. Baron William Lenore, Lothar had decided, was to become Elen's husband.

Another battle had broken out a scant month before her betrothal was to be decreed. The betrothal had never come to pass and William's whereabouts were presently unknown. She didn't know if her intended betrothed was dead, or alive and in hiding. She could only wish the marriage alliance had already come to pass so that William

Lenore might throw his soldiers behind Lothar in the fight to save their stronghold from barbarian hands.

That wasn't to be. And now, the saints save them all, it looked as though the most heavily fortified stronghold of Chippenham was a stone's throw from falling.

"Milady!"

Elen whirled around atop the parapet. She closed her eyes briefly and opened them on an expelling of air, grateful to see that her beloved nurse, Theodrada, was alive and well. Theodrada had been caring for her since she was but a babe, the elder woman now well into her forties.

Elen ran toward the woman. "Praise God Almighty you are well! What goes on below?" She felt desperate to hear that her brothers were alive. Her youngest brother, Arnulf, was deep within Wessex at the king's court, and therefore hopefully safe. Still, that left Lothar and Louis here in Chippenham, possible death lurking just around every corner. "Well?"

Theodrada's breathing was heavy, her blue eyes wide and haunted, as she stopped before her mistress and clutched at both of her arms. "Louis took a sword through the side, milady." She ignored the horrified cry from Elen and continued. "It looks deep, but mayhap the saints will smile on him. I packed the wound with herbs before I came to find you."

"And Lothar?"

The old woman shook her head. "I know naught of Lord Godeuart."

Elen felt ready to vomit. The temperature was nigh unto freezing atop the parapet due to a rogue January snow that had enveloped the region, yet her heart was pumping so mightily her forehead had broken out with beads of sweat. "Come!" she called out to Theodrada as she loosed from her hold. Grabbing her skirts, she ran from the tower into the keep proper. "We must aid them!"

"*We* must aid them?" the servant incredulously retorted as she followed on her mistress's heels. "Milady, we are but women. What are you thinking we can do?"

Elen didn't know, yet she felt sure they could do something. At this point their interference could hardly hurt.

"I know what to do!" she said, coming to a halt and whirling around to face Theodrada. Finally all the boring talk of battles she'd been subjected to over the years at countless feasts would serve her, and hopefully Lothar as well. "Gather me together five strong slaves and go to the kitchens the soonest."

"The kitchens?"

"Do not question me, Theodrada! Do as you are told!"

The servant inclined her head before dashing away. Elen ran as quickly as she could below stairs. Several minutes later, as Elen had known she would, Theodrada entered the kitchens with five of the Godeuarts' strongest slaves. Theodrada quirked a black eyebrow as she watched her mistress churn a cauldron of boiling hot wax over an open spit.

Elen's nostrils were flaring as she glanced up. Her outer

cloak had long since been removed, yet sweat plastered her modest green gown to her body from the labor of working the heavy spoon back and forth within the bubbling wax. She didn't care. Elen was tired of the bedamned Vikings, tired of losing men she loved to their greed and pilfering. King Alfred had paid them well to leave Wessex alone. The word-breakers had taken the offered Danegeld and agreed to return to Danish Mercia, a barbarian stronghold. They were liars, unholy savages, the lot of them.

"I need pitch and I need tar," Elen commanded the slaves without breaking from her task. "Get them and bring them to me anon."

Thirty minutes later, Elen smiled to herself as she watched the male Celtic slaves pour the wax, tar, and pitch concoction they'd created together into seven large urns, one for each of them. It took every bit of strength, grunting, and groaning Elen had in her to pick up her urn, but she was angry enough—and worried enough about her elder brother Lothar—to do it. "To the high walls!" she beseeched them. "Now!"

The slaves followed quickly, all of them as much in a frenzy as Elen to see their job done. They knew as well as their mistress did that should the keep fall to the Northmen, the Vikings were as likely to slay them all as they were to claim them for slaves of their own. All of their lives could very well depend on victory.

Elen's green eyes widened in horror as she glanced down the high wall and saw flaming arrows shooting toward the keep. Her heart beating rapidly, she instructed the slaves to set the urns down upon the wall until she signaled them to spill it upon the enemy below. That done, she frantically searched for Lothar. She didn't find him.

Nay! she thought, terrified. *Lothar—please be alive!*

Batting long blonde curls out of her line of vision, Elen got her first good look at the enemy. She stilled.

There were at least thirty of them and they had the keep surrounded on all sides. What's more, the Viking heathens were as huge and formidable as legend bespoke. They might have sat atop their warhorses, but even seated it was easy to surmise that not a one of them would be below six feet in height—most of them much taller.

All were heavily muscled, battle scars riddling their bronzed bodies, and bejeweled gold bangles delineating the musculature of their biceps. Many of them sported foreign braids plaited against either temple at the sides of the head—some even wore those braids in their beards.

They were the heathens King Alfred had called them. They were the nightmare the Church decreed them. They were the pestilence Lothar had sworn to destroy.

Elen's gaze collided with one of the Northmen's, a colossal barbarian who stood out from the other giants by virtue of the night-black hair that fell past his shoulders. He wore the same odd dress—bare chest despite the freezing weather, leather brais, gold bangles clasped unforgivingly about either arm, and two braids plaiting the hair back from his temples. There the similarities ended. Most of the others were fair of hair and eye. This warlord's hair was darker even than the Welsh Theodrada, his eyes a chilling, fathomless black.

Elen shivered. The savage looked ruthless, merciless.

He held his sword high into the air and bellowed a war cry that sent a deeper chill coursing down the length of her spine. His men responded to whatever heathen word he'd yelled, and two warriors on horseback came charging toward the front of the circle, a battering ram held between them.

Sweet saints—nay!

Terror quickly evolved into anger. Her jaw clenching, Elen stared challengingly down to the black-haired Viking as her hands seized either side of the urn. His dark gaze narrowed as he wondered at her intentions.

"Now!" Elen called out to the slaves, her eyes never leaving the barbarian's. "Kill them all!"

She had assumed the savage wouldn't understand her tongue. She had been wrong.

The giant's eyes widened as he watched Elen and the Godeuart slaves pick up the urns and prepare to heave them over the high walls. He called out a warning to the others as he backed up his warhorse—bedamn the heathen to the fires of hell anyway! Yet much to Elen's satisfaction, the warning hadn't come in time to save them all.

In fact, she thought, her breath shuddering as the feeling of victory surged through her and warmed her, the Viking's warning hadn't saved nigh unto a dozen of them.

The two warriors with the battering ram fell screaming to the ground on contact!

The warlord cursed as pandemonium broke out around him. Warriors were screaming, their scalps and backs burning, as boiled wax, tar, and pitch clung to them, the concoction refusing to let go. Three more men collapsed in agony. Several more threw themselves to the snow-dusted ground and wallowed around in it like helpless pigs, screaming as the brew ate at their flesh.

Elen smiled with a satisfaction that bordered on maniacal hysteria, her gaze straying back to the warlord staring daggers at her. These barbarians had killed her sire, injured her cherished younger brother Louis, and the saints only knew what horrors had befallen her beloved elder brother, Lothar. To her way of the thinking, the Northmen had this day coming—and then some.

"Die!" Elen spat, tears that refused to fall springing to her eyes. In that moment, all of her fear, all of her rage, and all of her hatred coalesced into a warbled cry that reached the earshot of the mammoth giant whose soulless black eyes tracked her every movement. "I pray to the heavens that every last one of you *die!*"

Time stood still as the Saxon lady and the Viking warlord stared each other down. Both sets of eyes were narrowed, both sets of nostrils flaring, and both jaws clenched. Elen's heart drummed in her chest.

She shivered as it occurred to her that the warlord was assessing her as though he mayhap wanted to kill her with his bare hands for this slight. It was of no consequence. Were Louis and Lothar to die, Elen thought it just as well to join them.

Long moments ticked by. Carnage and mayhem surrounded them; screams permeated the air. And then, finally, after what felt like long hours, the raven-haired warlord broke Elen's stare. Bellowing a foreign word that she took to mean retreat or something equivalent, she watched with satisfaction and elation as the Northman and his surviving men rode off from the keep and away from Chippenham.

Her breath caught in the back of her throat. Elen clutched her stomach and gasped, the reality of what she'd just accomplished catching up to her as she used a shaking hand to support herself against the wall.

She had done it. Her plan had worked.

"Milady!" Theodrada laughed, her hands clutching either of Elen's shoulders. "You saved us all! I can scarce believe it, yet I saw the savages retreat with mine own eyes!"

"I know," Elen rasped, her gaze round and disbelieving. "It worked," she added in a dumbfounded murmur. "Praise the saints."

Theodrada's chuckle deepened. She hugged her mistress tightly to her. "Because of you, my heart. All because of you!"

Elen's thoughts briefly returned to the chilling black eyes that belonged to a certain Viking. She swallowed over a lump of worry in her throat, stark fear that he would seek retribution momentarily overtaking her.

She discarded the thought almost as quickly as it came to her. There would be no sense in attempting yet another raid on the keep. The barbarians were removed from their stronghold in Danish Mercia. They would return there. By the time they came back with reinforcements—if indeed they ever returned with reinforcements—Elen would see to it that the keep was a veritable fortress.

Elen's smile came slowly, but when it came it was luminous. "We did it," she breathed. She began to laugh, dancing around with an elated Theodrada. She was certain her father could see her from the heavens and that he was smiling down upon her. "We won!"

Tired and bone-weary, Elen paid no attention to the girl washing her hair. Her thoughts were miles away, or more to the point, four rooms and one floor away.

Her younger brother Louis's injury was far more severe than what Theodrada had informed her of atop the parapet. She supposed Theodrada, someone she thought of more as mother than servant, had told Elen what she thought she needed to hear to endure until the Vikings had retreated.

Mayhap Theodrada had the right of it. Mayhap Elen would have been too overwrought with grief to keep her wits about her had she known her beloved Louis would be dead by morn. And then all would have been lost to them— the keep, their way of life, mayhap even their very lives.

Lothar, her elder brother and lord of the Godeuart estate, had taken a large gash to the shoulder. He wasn't looking too well himself, yet he did seem to be faring far better than young Louis. She could only pray Lothar survived his injuries. Elen wasn't certain she could bear it were she to lose two brothers within one eve. And, she realized, tears gathering in her eyes, only a miracle from the angels could save Louis now.

Seated naked in a barrel with lukewarm water insulating her from the cold bedchamber, Elen brought her knees up closer to her chest and tightly wrapped her arms around them. Her brothers oft teased her that she wasn't given to weeping at the drop of a hat like 'twas said females are wont to do.

Mayhap not in front of others. Yet there were many an eve after Papa died, like tonight, when Elen took to her chamber and wept until her head ached.

Papa, why did you have to die? Why! I am so alone and so terribly frightened!

"Milady?" the sweet-tempered twelve-year-old slave, Marda, whispered. She stilled her hands in Elen's wet hair. "Milady, what ails you?"

Elen thought to comfort her, for the distress in the child's voice was obvious, but by then she was weeping uncontrollably, her body shaking and nigh unto convulsing from the violence of it. And really what could she say to young Marda? Only things the girl already knew.

She missed Papa. She knew in her heart Louis would be

dead by morn. Lothar might possibly die too. And all because of the bedamned Vikings and their heartless greed!

Elen's nostrils flared as the tears, little by little, dried up.
Hatred and rage coalesced once again just as it had out on
the parapet.

To hell with the savages! To hell with every last bloody
one of them!

Her only consolation, Elen knew, was that some of the
heathens had died amidst their pilfering. But not enough.
Nay, not nearly enough.

Chapter 2

"I wish no part in this!" the warlord Amund bellowed to another Viking leader called Guthorm. "Mercia is ours and my warriors wish to settle it. You waste our time and valuable Viking lives with talk of overtaking Wessex. Loki keep it—I don't covet the wretched place!"

Ivar Hrolf's gaze flicked from his half-brother Amund to the frowning Guthorm. Guthorm was a formidable leader and a warrior who wanted to see their people conquer the whole of Saxony. Ivar doubted Guthorm would put down his sword and call peace the soonest; he would return to Chippenham and besiege it before conquering the whole of Wessex.

Ivar was of a mind to settle in the Viking-controlled Mercia like his brother, yet could he also see the sense in Guthorm's plan. The Saxon king, Alfred, had shown his idiocy when first he had offered Danegeld in exchange for the warriors' leave-taking from Wessex. A true leader would have fought to the bitter end in the name of his people and land. The weakling Alfred was undeserving of his title.

Mayhap Guthorm should be made the king of Wessex. Ivar didn't care which of the warriors prevailed and ruled there, only that a Viking claimed it for his own.

Until last eve, Ivar had wanted no more a part in returning to Chippenham than Amund did. Ivar possessed, after all, his own stronghold in Mercia and nigh unto thirty slaves to see to his bidding. He wanted to settle his new lands as much as Amund did. He did not need or covet the Chippenham stronghold—until last eve.

But then until last eve Ivar had never watched an icily beautiful wench all but single-handedly defeat a Viking raid party. That was a slight that could not be let go.

"I will go with Guthorm."

All eyes in the long hall turned to Ivar. Amund frowned. "What nonsense talk is this? Until the raid on Chippenham you—"

"The whispers have reached our ears already, brother." Ivar's jaw tensed. "I've no desire to go further into Wessex than the border town of Chippenham. I leave the rest of Wessex to Guthorm. I will return to Mercia upon claiming the Chippenham stronghold for mine own." His next words were slow, methodical. "And upon claiming a certain 'lady' as mine own slave."

Amund grinned, his gaze flicking back and forth between his brother and Ivar's men. "She is a lady. Tempting though it might be, especially considering she is but a lowly Saxon, you cannot enslave a wench of gentle breeding. Were it done to one of our own, we'd demand vengeance and rightly so."

"She killed ten of our men and maimed two more," Ivar murmured, the reminder forcing the smile from Amund's lips. "With her own two cunning hands." His face didn't betray emotion, yet his eyes were blazing, the muscles of his biceps bulging with barely controlled fury. "She is no gentle lady," Ivar bit out. "She is a devil spawned of Loki." Beautiful she might be, but it was but a ruse to cover up the demon within. "She *will* be my slave."

Silence.

"Very well," Amund conceded. "Follow Guthorm to Chippenham. Conquer it and take your woman—"

Ivar slowly shook his head. His black eyes narrowed. "My slave, not my woman."

"Take your *slave* then," Amund overenunciated. He frowned. "But be quick about returning to Mercia. I give you leave to be gone but a fortnight. After that, you are to exert your control as lord over the lands I have given to you. I will not have the people there forgetting that our kind now rule them."

Ivar nodded. Memories of last eve flooded through his mind. She had wanted them to die—all of them. Were she a man, he would have paid her back by the taking of her life. Instead she would serve him until she took her last breath—in the bedsheets and out of them.

"I need but a sennight," Ivar murmured. "One week and she—and Chippenham—will be mine."

"They haven't had the time to rebuild," Ivar coldly predicted as he walked a wide circle around the seated warriors. He was as well known in Saxony as he was in the Northlands for his ruthlessness, for his willingness to overpower at all costs. Yet not even those who most feared Ivar Hrolf would believe any warlord could rebound in such a short amount of time. "Chippenham will never expect us to return within three eves."

Guthorm frowned. "That fortress is made of stone. Rarely do we come across such a keep as that one. Our arrows were of no consequence. A new plan is needed."

Ivar inclined his head. "And I've one at the ready."

"Go on."

Ivar continued his wide stride around the seated warriors. He wanted to proceed the soonest, conquer the soonest, and return to Mercia and his beloved adopted Jorvik the soonest. "Those stones are impenetrable mayhap, but smooth they are not."

Guthorm's face scrunched up. "Eh?"

Ivar ran a hand over his jaw, his expression intense. "The stones aren't cut smooth. There is plenty of space for foot notches upon each one."

"You wish to go in quiet?" Ivar's man Olaf inquired. "Lay siege from within instead of from without?"

"Aye."

Olaf nodded, impressed. "A worthy plan of attack, milord."

"Surprise is on our side and will work to our advantage," Ivar concluded.

"As are the gods," Guthorm barked. He spat on the ground, his eyes narrowed. "The savage, smelly Saxons will lay at our feet like the dogs they are before the sennight passes!"

Cheers erupted. "Yea" and "praise Odin" echoed throughout the long hall.

Barely clad female slaves scurried to refill trenchers and goblets. Guthorm kept his most buxom and beautiful slaves in so little clothing that Ivar wasn't at all surprised when one bent over to fill a trencher and he could see from behind what she had to offer between her legs.

Ivar's eyelids grew heavy with arousal as he stared at the thrall's pretty pink pussy. She wasn't so beautiful of face as Ivar's soon-to-be slave was, but she would do for an eve. He found himself wondering if Guthorm was of a mind to share one of his thralls.

As if he'd read his thoughts, Guthorm winked at Ivar. "Enjoy," he chuckled, standing up to retire to his chamber until morn. "Her cunt is all yours tonight."

* * *

Ivar spent three hours riding the luscious slave's body like a man possessed, then another four hours sleeping. The warriors took to their mounts early the next morn, determined to reach Wessex by sunset.

As the Viking entourage stealthily made its way toward Chippenham, Ivar felt the familiar surge of impending conquest course through his blood. He hadn't given much thought to the witch of Wessex after declaring to his brother she would become his slave, for after that Ivar had been too preoccupied deciding on strategy to give the wench herself much thought. But now as they rode, their plan of attack firmly ingrained, he had time to think on her, to dwell on what she'd done.

He'd never seen a woman like that one—never. He half hated her and, he begrudgingly admitted to himself, half admired her. But admiration or no, that witch was responsible for his brother Agnar's incapacitation. She might not have been the one who heaved the brew that maimed him, yet she had definitely been the one who gave the order to her thralls to do as much. *"Kill them all!"* she had raged. *"Die!"*

All he could think about now was that wench, the witch who would soon be his to do with what he would. Ivar cared not about controlling Chippenham—he would leave some warriors there to ensure its subjugation, but his main goal was the wench.

He wanted to make her pay for the ten deaths and two maimings she'd brought to his people. Ivar had seen warriors as cunning and deadly as the Chippenham lady, but never had he witnessed such a thing in a wench. She was an abomination. To the Saxon one-god and to the Viking gods who ruled Valhalla alike—she was an abomination of all that was sacred.

Ivar found himself looking forward to bringing her to heel, his heel. He was enjoying the mental image perhaps more than he should have. His blood shouldn't boil with need at the thought of claiming her as his chattel, yet it did. His cock shouldn't be stone-hard at contemplating all the wicked ways she would serve him, especially as well-used as it was from last eve, yet it was.

"They say," Guthorm informed him on a chuckle as they rode side by side on their destriers, "that witches who belong to the Saxon devil make for great bedsport." He grinned as Ivar's men chuckled with him. "Lucky Viking dog."

Ivar snorted at that. "I cannot imagine a wench so icy as that one will make for much amusement in the bed-sheets."

"Should be fun to thaw her out, though," Ivar's man, Olaf, quipped, earning him a few guffaws. "Lick her 'til she melts!"

"*Mmmm mmm mmm,*" Guthorm said, wagging his bushy eyebrows. "I can't say I'd mind being the one to lick her all over. Evil she might be, but a finer wench the gods have never made."

All the more reason she was an abomination to Ivar's way of thinking. Like the song of the buxom sea creatures that lured seafarers to their early demise, the wench was beautiful, but she was also deadly.

Ivar turned his concentration back to the task at hand, his muscles cording in reaction to the impending raid. By morn word would go out that the Vikings had seized Chippenham, that their lady had been enslaved, and that all of Wessex would be brought under Viking dominion.

Ivar didn't care about the rest of Saxony. He cared only of Chippenham.

And of enslaving the witch of Wessex.

Lady Elen gently patted her brother Lothar's head with a wet cloth, her heart in her eyes as she tended to him. Their younger brother Louis had died of his injuries last eve. She had held him tightly, sobbing onto his chest as he'd passed from this life and moved on to the next. Elen had begged him not to leave them as she told Louis of her love for him, but in the end the choice hadn't been his to make.

Louis Godeuart, fourteen, was dead. Her younger brother, her father—both dead at the hands of savages. Now all that was left of the Godeuarts were Lothar, Arnulf, and Elen. And Lothar she couldn't be certain of.

"Your injury is not nearly so deep as Louis's was," Elen murmured, a reassuring smile forming on her lips. "You will heal. Of this I am certain," she lied.

Lying was a sin, mayhap, but in this instance she decided it was less a sin than the truth. Later she would beseech the priests for forgiveness. This eve she would tell Lothar any lie he needed to lift his spirits.

"I—I'm sorry I did not protect you, Elen," Lothar weakly mumbled. "I—"

"Shhh," she softly chastised. She bent her neck to kiss his forehead. "You were outnumbered. You fought hard and made Papa proud. No man could have stood against such numbers save God himself."

"But you did," Lothar whispered. He found his first smile, though Elen could tell it pained him to make one. "If Papa is proud of me, he is fair bursting with pride at you."

Elen's chuckle was soft. "Desperate times call for desperate actions. 'Twas no more cunning than that. Now be quiet and rest before I tar you, too," she teased.

He snorted at that—then winced from the pain the slight action caused. He offered no resistance when his sister held a chalice to his lips and ordered him to drink.

A few minutes later, Elen sighed as she watched her brother fall into a deep sleep from the herbs in the mead she'd given him to drink. She hadn't slept in days and the fatigue was at last catching up to her. Tired or not, she refused to leave Lothar's side. Her brother needed her. And so long as Lothar required her support and aid, she would be there to give it to him.

A chill worked up and down Elen's spine, the sort of eerie foreboding one experiences when they sense they are being watched. She glanced up and saw no one, so she shook the feeling off. She turned her attention back to her brother.

Elen's hand shook as she reached out to Lothar. She didn't know whether the trembling was born of fatigue, fear of his possible death, or both. Her fingertips lightly brushed over a lock of dark gold hair plastered to her brother's forehead from sweat.

"Please come back to me," Elen whispered, tears that did not fall gathered in her eyes. "Do not leave me alone, Lothar. We are all the other has left." Her breath caught in the back of her throat. "Please do not leave me—I love you."

The doors to the chamber came crashing open, startling Elen. She jumped to her feet, whirling around to face the intruders. The skirt of her costly, green woolen gown swirled in time with the movement, long golden curls cascading down her back and over her shoulders.

"Who goes there?" she furiously whispered. She didn't want anyone disturbing Lothar's healing sleep. He needed every moment of it.

Never one with much talent for divining more than silhouettes from nigh unto darkness, the single candle burning at Lothar's bedside was not enough to aid her. She bent to light another one, then held the beeswax candle up so she could see which serf it was she would be taking to task.

Elen's breathing stilled. Her heart all but stopped.

There was no serf standing there. There were free men—five huge, unsmiling men who had no business being in Lothar's bedchamber. And one of those men, Elen thought, swallowing roughly as their gazes clashed, was far too familiar for her peace of mind.

He was as heavy with muscle as he was long with height. Gold bangles clasped around each bulging bicep, strong thighs showed even from beneath the brais he wore. His eyes were blacker than the tar she'd used against him three days hence, and just as fathomless. There was no mercy in those eyes, no sense of compassion or pity. There was only ruthlessness—a desire to win at all costs.

Sweet saints above. The heathen had come back. And somehow Elen knew—*knew*—he'd come back for her.

This isn't possible! I've heard no cry-outs from the servants let alone the clanging of swords!

"Nay," she gasped, unthinkingly backing up until she all but stumbled into her brother's bed.

Her green eyes widened with horror as she watched the black-haired giant of a warlord look his fill at her body before turning his attention to her face. Her heart was beating so rapidly she felt certain she might swoon then and there. "Ah God—nay!"

Chapter 3

"Kill him," Ivar coldly instructed his man Olaf, motioning with his head toward the witch's felled lover. Ivar spoke in Saxon, that the wench would know his intentions. She cried out as he'd supposed she would, her hand flying up to shield her mouth.

Jealousy and rage the likes of which he'd never before experienced assaulted Ivar the very moment he'd witnessed the icy witch speak so sweetly to her injured lover. Watching her all but cry now, knowing her Saxon co-conspirator was about to be put to his death, only made the jealousy that much more acute. Ridiculous, mayhap, yet Ivar considered her to be his. For much longer than he felt comfortable remembering.

'Twas of no consequence. What was of consequence in the here and the now was that she could kill ten Vikings and smile. The death of her lover, however, made her ice melt. Ivar's jaw clenched.

"Please—nay!" the witch cried out. Her voice trembled as she pleaded with him. "I beg you to spare his life, milord!"

Ivar's nostrils flared as they once again locked gazes. "Kill him," he softly repeated to Olaf without glancing away. "Now."

The witch began to sob as she ran across the chamber and threw herself prostrate at Ivar's feet. "I—I—nay!" she cried.

She sounded a bit hysterical and, despite the jealousy he was experiencing, Ivar felt something inside the vicinity of his heart soften just a bit. He had never thought to see a wench so cold as this one melt for any man. He had expected her to plead for her own life, but not for the life of any other.

The wench threw her arms around Ivar's calves and looked up to him with tears in her eyes. "My lord, I beg you to spare my brother! Kill me for your retribution if you must, but please—show mercy to my brother!"

Ivar stilled. Learning that the felled man was the witch's brother served to lessen his jealousy, but not the barely controlled rage that bubbled just below the surface. "The same as you showed mercy to my brother?" he hissed.

She stilled. Wide green eyes flew up and then narrowed as she swiped a tear from her cheek using the back of her hand. "You attacked my home, warlord. I defend what's mine."

A dark eyebrow quirked. "Yours? If your brother is abed still alive, this keep is not yours but his."

"It's my home," she said calmly, but with a sense of love and loyalty that could not be mistaken. She rose to her feet and straightened her spine. "I defend what's mine."

Admiration. There it was again. He squelched the traitorous feeling, recalling the maimed brother who lay abed.

"It's no longer yours," Ivar murmured, making her eyes round once again. "This keep and all of Chippenham are now mine."

She visibly shivered, yet her pride would not allow her to betray further fear. Ivar supposed she was wondering just how the keep had been seized when no battling had transpired.

This time the Vikings had besieged the stronghold from the inside out rather than from the outside in. It took but one well-aimed arrow through the heart to kill the lookout atop the parapet, and the rest had been like child's play. Scaling the walls had taken even less effort than Ivar had supposed it would. The walls were made of stone, but as he predicted, their weakness was in their lack of smoothness.

Her face pinched with fear, the witch backed away from Ivar and returned to her brother's bedside. "Kill us then and be done with it," she spat, the hatred and determination he'd witnessed in her atop the wall at last rearing its head. "Lothar would rather die than be subjugated to barbarians and your heathen gods—as would I!"

Ivar's black eyes gleamed. "You do not decide your fate, slave," he said softly. "Your Master decides it."

Her lips worked up and down but no words came out as Ivar's intentions at last dawned on her and took hold. She gasped.

"B–But I am a lady," she breathed out. "Lady Elen of Godeuart. Surely not even a savage would mean to—"

"I mean to," he murmured. His jaw tightened as he glanced around the bedchamber before returning his gaze to his captive. "You best take a long, hard look at that pretty gown you are wearing, slave. It'll be the last time you see a garment for a long time—if ever again."

Silence.

The witch's eyes rolled back into her head precisely one second before she swooned. Olaf chuckled as he watched Ivar sweep her limp form up into his arms.

Ivar glared at him. "There is something amusing?"

"Nay," Olaf snorted. "There is nothing amusing at all about watching a wench faint dead away at the thought of you mounting her."

The other three warriors had a laugh at that. Ivar didn't smile, but he was well humored. "Mayhap she was overcome with gratitude," he quipped back.

Olaf wiped tears of humor from his eyes. "Aye," Olaf laughed. "Mayhap so."

* * *

'Twould take five days journey to reach the enemy's stronghold. Thankfully, Elen had been given leave to care for her sorely injured brother during the trek. Due to Lothar's shoulder wound, and unlike the other men and women taken as slaves by the barbarians, Elen and Lothar were permitted to ride in the wagon instead of having to walk beside it.

The barbarian warlord, whom Elen had since learned was called Ivar Hrolf, had gratefully kept his distance from her so far. The first eve they made camp, Elen was left to sleep beside Lothar in the wagon, though Viking guards slept around it, ensuring that she wouldn't escape.

As if she could leave her brother behind. Nay, she would rather die with him than leave him to savages.

Elen suspected the barbarian, Ivar, realized that to be true. She couldn't fathom another reason that he would be troubled to bring an injured and mayhap dying Saxon lord with him. It only made the journey that much slower and longer. Unless, of course, he meant to barter Lothar for more Danegeld from King Alfred. Lothar was, after all, one of the king's most trusted nobles.

The Viking had left her alone thus far, yet occasionally Elen had caught him stealing glances at her. She didn't know if he did so to keep a watchful eye over his captive or because he was contemplating all the godless things he meant to do to her.

He meant to make her a whore. The whore of a dog.

She hated him. Her stomach fair expelled itself just thinking of the giant taking her as a bed slave. Elen hadn't much knowledge—any knowledge really—of what a bed slave did, but she was certain she wouldn't have a care for it. She was worldly enough and had been possessed of brothers long enough to realize that whatever it was men did with bed slaves it would put an illegitimate babe in her belly.

Verily, she knew of at least two babes the bed slave Hilda had bore her brother Lothar. Hilda had been a slave from birth to when she died bearing Lothar's second daughter. Lothar had not been permitted by their father to take Hilda to wife, yet he had made it known to their sire and throughout Chippenham that his daughters were not slaves and hence were not to be treated thusly. Papa had respected Lothar's wishes.

Hate was not a strong enough word for her captor, Elen decided. The Vikings were responsible for the death of her father, the death of her brother Louis, and quite possibly the death of Lothar. Now the giant savage meant to enslave her, too.

Elen had trouble sleeping that first eve even though her brother slept quietly beside her. The still of the night gave her too much time to think, too much time to remember that the grim Ivar Hrolf planned to make a bed slave out of her.

It was humiliation. Sheer, unadulterated humiliation.

Her cheeks fair flamed with embarrassment at knowing her fate. No man save a savage would make a slave out of a lady.

Elen stared at nothing, her eyes unblinking. She would be no man's slave.

Not now. Not ever.

By the second day of their journey, Lothar was swimming in and out of pained consciousness. The small moans made Elen wince for her brother, yet she was glad to hear them for it meant he was on the mend. At least, that's what she hoped.

"Elen," Lothar weakly rasped. "Elen."

"Shhh, I am here," she whispered, keeping her voice a hush as she bent her neck and kissed him. She didn't want the Vikings to know her brother had awakened. She feared they might purposely injure him further, torture him in the name of Lord Hrolf's maimed brother, Agnar.

"Elen," Lothar muttered.

Sweat slicked his forehead. She feared the icy wind hitting him there would give him a fever he would never recover from, so she quickly wrapped a fresh wool blanket around him.

"Shhh! I am here, brother. I beg you to rest."

"Elen," he mumbled, ignoring her. "You must find the king."

Her eyes widened. Lothar's voice was so weak as to be barely audible, yet she'd heard his command without trouble.

"Escape?" she whispered. Elen stilled. "I cannot leave you, Lothar. I cannot—"

"Elen, please," Lothar rasped. "I'm already dead. They will kill me do I not die from my affliction. This you know."

She closed her eyes against his words. Pain clawed at her gut. Hatred seethed through her blood.

"B–But my daughters. And Wessex . . ."

His unfinished sentence hung there between them. If Elen didn't escape and warn the king, Alfred might not know Chippenham had fallen until it was too late, until the savages had wreaked havoc on the king's own stronghold deep in Wessex.

The entire kingdom could fall. Every gently bred lady stood to be reduced to the status of a barbarian's bed slave, every nobleman put to his death. And her nieces—

Sweet saints, she could not let that happen to them.

"I love you, Lothar," Elen quietly gasped. "I love you so much it fair hurts."

It took every bit of strength her brother had to smile up to his sister, but he did. "I know, Elen. As I love you. Flee this eve as the Vikings slumber. Find William Lenore. He will take you to the king does he live." He winced, the pain jarring. "Flee knowing I will always love you." He grabbed for the sleeve of her cloak, though his grasp was weak.

"Swear to me now you will go, Elen. Swear it by Wessex and Alfred."

Most noblemen didn't place merit in the sworn word of a wench. Lothar did. Yet one more reason to love him as she did.

She was quiet for a long moment, and then, "I swear it." Elen took a deep breath and slowly expelled it. "By King Alfred and mighty Wessex I swear to escape do I die in the trying."

"No dying," Lothar murmured, his eyes closing to rest. "Just escape."

Chapter 4

Elen's eyes widened in shock as she watched four naked Viking warriors emerge from a nearby—and icy cold—body of water. She wasn't certain if she was more taken aback by the fact they'd bathed in such freezing weather or that they weren't even trying to conceal their manparts from her.

Elen knew there were differences between males and females that went beyond height and muscles. She just hadn't known that certain parts on a man got so long, and so swoon-inducingly thick.

Lord Hrolf walked over to stand in front of the wagon, his dark eyes never leaving Elen. She gulped as her worried gaze flicked up and down the length of his steel-hard body, simultaneously praying this eve would not be the night the savage decided to make bedsport out of her. She expelled a breath of tentative relief when he made no motion to manhandle her.

Sweet saints but Elen was suddenly glad Lothar had commanded her to flee! Knowing what she did now about barbarian manparts, she vowed she would never become a bed slave to this one. She would die first. Then again, she thought, her jaw dropping as she watched Lord Hrolf's manpart grow impossibly longer and thicker, she would mayhap die anyway.

"Why does it do that?" Elen asked without thinking as the Viking dried himself off using a fresh blanket. She was too stunned to consider the impropriety of her words—or her gawking.

The savage smiled—an event as noteworthy as that manpart of his that could grow of its own volition. His smile served to shake the cobwebs from Elen's mind, forcing her to recall the fact that she was asking questions about something she didn't want to know the answers to now or ever. Forcing her, too, to remember that she hated him and the whole of his kind. Her eyes narrowed.

"Never mind," she said haughtily, glancing away. She pulled the blankets tighter around her before looking back to her captor. " 'Tis no concern nor care of mine."

His voice was thick, his eyes hooded. "He grows because he wants you," Lord Hrolf murmured.

The smile was mayhap gone, but Elen warily noted

she still held his rapt interest. "He?" she asked. Her lips pursed. "What mean you that he—" She stilled, then cleared her throat. "Oh," she said dumbly, her cheeks suffused with heat.

That bedamned smile again. This time Elen noted a small dimple denting one cheek. She quickly looked away.

He was a handsome man, she begrudgingly admitted to herself. Had her captor been a Saxon noble who had peacefully ridden into Chippenham to request her hand in marriage from Lothar, she would like as not have swooned with giddy happiness at her good fortune. But Lord Ivar Hrolf was no Saxon nobleman held in high esteem by King Alfred and Wessex. He was a godless heathen, a savage who meant to enslave her and her people.

"Come here," Lord Hrolf instructed.

His voice was hoarse, the tone of his words foreign enough to Elen that she glanced up to see what ailed him. Her eyes bulged in fright when she saw that his manpart had swelled nigh unto the size of a child's arm. A plump child at that.

"By the saints," she muttered, her words tripping out one after the other, "just kill me now rather than split me asunder."

He grinned. She gulped.

"I take care of my chattel," Lord Hrolf murmured. "I won't hurt you."

Elen's teeth gritted at his use of the word *chattel*, a not so subtle reminder as to her new and unwanted status. His black gaze saw everything, she was certain. She doubted she'd managed to school her features before the savage realized he'd gotten to her. She supposed her clenched jaw and venomous expression could give her feelings away to any imbecile. And an imbecile he was not.

"Shouldn't you retrieve your garments before that thing of yours freezes up and falls off?" she bit out. Her nostrils flared as she glanced away. "Not that I'd care if it did, mind you."

His eyebrows shot up as he otherwise ignored her words. "Come here," he said again, holding out his hand. "Now."

Elen hesitated as her heart began to pound in her chest.

"Now, Elen," the warlord said in a harder, louder voice. "Do not make me ask again."

She wet her parched lips and glanced down to Lothar. If the Viking's words grew louder he would like as not wake up her brother. And Lothar, maimed or not, would try to defend his sister from their captor's assault.

Lothar could not possibly survive. Not now. Not in his weakened state.

She ignored her hastily beating heart, ignored too the lightheadedness that threatened to make her swoon, and scooted off the wagon that she might stand before the warlord. Her gaze downcast, she said nothing, only stood there and, seething with fury, waited his next instruction.

Taking her by the hand, Lord Hrolf led his frightened captive into a nearby tent. After barking at a grinning Olaf to get out, he shooed Elen inside and let the flap fall shut.

"I will not be mounting you this eve," her captor remarked as he turned away from her and lit a beeswax candle inside the animal hide tent. "So calm yourself."

Elen's expression was at once angry and more than a bit nervous. Her gaze trailed from his chiseled buttocks to the wide and scarred expanse of his massive back. She licked her dry lips. "Then why bring me in here?"

He turned around on his knees, giving Elen her first look at his front in fairly good lighting. Her jaw took to dropping again as she couldn't help but to stare.

His rod was long and thick, and jutted up to his navel from a nest of curls as black as the hair atop his head. A thin line of dark hair trailed up from his navel and toward a chest as huge, defined, and battle-scarred as his back.

Her gaze drifted upward to a masculinely elegant neck, then farther up to a face that was as chiseled and rugged as it was primal and beautiful. Or it would have been, Elen forced herself to recall as she coughed into her hand and glanced away, had it not belonged to a barbarian savage.

"I brought you in here to feed you," Lord Hrolf told her. One eyebrow rose. "Olaf informed me that you have not eaten since this morn."

"I wasn't hungry," she said quietly, her gaze still turned away. "And I'm still not. May I return to my brother?" she asked in a small, hopeful voice.

"Nay."

Her heart sank. She had known before asking that would be his answer, yet she'd permitted herself one last hope at being able to escape before the warlord split her asunder with that wicked beast of a thing.

Elen folded her hands in her lap with what she hoped looked like gentle patience, her gaze cast toward the ground. "May I leave after I eat?"

"Aye."

Hope surged anew.

"Take your dress off."

Hope plummeted anew.

"I thought you didn't mean to mount me this eve," she breathed out.

"I do not."

Her forehead wrinkled as she at last glanced up. "Savages eat naked?" she asked incredulously.

He didn't so much as crack a smile, yet she saw amusement there in his eyes. "Of course," he drawled. "Don't the savage Saxons eat naked?"

She gasped at the slight. "Nay! And we are not the savages!"

"You've lesser weapons, lesser armies, and lesser ways. Savages, I daresay."

Elen had no rejoinder to that. The Vikings had, in fact, bested the Saxon armies on more occasions than she felt comfortable recalling. "Well," she snapped, "at least we've the sense to wear clothing in the dead of winter. And not to eat naked!"

That bedamned smile again, she noted. Followed by that bedamned dimple.

"Eating naked is far superior to eating clothed."

She frowned. "I somehow doubt that."

A dark eyebrow quirked. "Then you have eaten naked before to know this?"

"Well, not precisely, yet am I certain—"

"Take your clothes off," Lord Hrolf murmured. His voice grew thick again, his gaze once more taking on that drugged look. "Now."

Elen hesitated. She worried her bottom lip. Thoughts of hatred and escape momentarily fled as she concentrated on the frightening aspects of the present.

"Now," he softly but firmly repeated. "Do as I tell you, Elen."

She took a deep breath and shakily blew it out. She wanted to run—to scream and refuse his order—yet also did she see the wisdom in letting the brute think she was quick to demure.

'Twould be that much more the shock when she ran.

And oh how she would enjoy besting the savage! She hated his murdering kind—and him in particular. Mayhap Louis and Papa would smile down upon her from the heavens when the Viking marauder was bested by her.

Mentally conceding that she didn't have much of a choice, Elen prepared to obey Lord Hrolf's command. Refusing to look at her captor, her jaw tightened as she removed her outer cloak and tossed it behind her.

"Now the boots."

The boots were next discarded. They were her best pair so she was careful to set them down with care, though the thought of hurling them at the grim-faced beast was fair tempting.

"And your gown," he said hoarsely.

Elen closed her eyes briefly, willing herself not to blush. She would show no weakness to this Viking.

Reaching for the skirt of her green dress, her eyelids drifted open. She pulled the hem up above her head and struggled with the garment. Her breasts were on the large side, and so got caught up in the wool a disgruntling moment, but finally they sprang free.

Her will not to blush lasted until the moment she heard the Viking's breath suck in. She couldn't be certain what such a sound signified—disgust or desire—yet both possible results disheartened her.

Disgust because it injured her pride even if she shouldn't care. Desire because it meant she wouldn't leave the tent a virgin and any hope at a marriage with William Lenore would be vanquished.

"Lie down on your side."

Her eyes rounded. "But I thought—"

"A slave does not question her Master. You best learn that now, Elen, for any hope at happiness."

Her pride smarted at his use of the word *slave,* but she took to her side and lay on the animal pelt–covered ground without further comment. Her skin began to goosepimple and her nipples stiffened to the point of aching from the chill in the ground, which the animal pelts only minimally thwarted.

"I'll have you warm in a moment, my beautiful Elen," Lord Hrolf murmured, apparently noting how cold she was.

He turned on his side, too, so that he faced her, then reached to a place between them and above his head where Elen noticed food for the first time. Bread. Mutton. Cheese. Even a tart. Her mouth watered, hunger pangs assaulting her for the first time since her detainment.

Her captor placed a tiny wedge of cheese between a thumb and forefinger then held it to her lips. "Open your mouth," he softly instructed her.

When her full lips parted, he placed the tangy bit of cheese on her tongue. His gaze watched her mouth as she slowly chewed. She nervously swallowed, her eyes widening when his finger gently traced the outline of her lips. The sensation did an odd thing to her belly, making it clench in an uncomfortable and foreign way.

"Like silk," he murmured. His dark eyes trailed down to her breasts. "Lie on your back," he said thickly. "It's my turn to eat."

She blinked, not understanding what that had to do with lying on her back, but she did as she'd been bade without questioning him. Elen watched the Viking place food bits all over her body. A wedge of cheese on each jutting nipple. A piece of bread on her belly. And, she blushed, a bit of tart on her golden-curled mons.

Savages, she determined, had decidedly embarrassing eating habits.

Despite her resolve not to question him, Elen opened her mouth to do just that. She found breath rushing from her throat instead of words, however, when a strong, warm tongue curled around one achingly stiff nipple and drew it into a hot mouth, cheese bit and all.

He apparently wolfed the cheese wedge down quickly, for one moment it was there and the next her nipple was being licked and lavished with nothing guarding mouth from flesh. She whimpered as teeth and tongue tugged at her nipple before his demanding mouth suckled it.

Elen moaned, the odd clenching of her belly growing worse. Fire sizzled through her blood as her head lulled back and her breathing grew heavy and labored. By the time her captor's mouth claimed the other bit of cheese, her body was fair screaming for—something. She knew not what, only that she felt as though there was more to the sensations than this.

Lord Hrolf's breathing looked to be as heavy as her own, Elen thought, as she watched his chiseled chest rise and fall through hooded eyes. Trapping her bodily beneath him, he used his knee to separate her thighs and settle himself just above her.

Elen's breathing stilled. The Viking's mouth dove for her navel, the bread there quickly chewed and swallowed. She panted for air as his tongue swirled around her belly, licking around her navel before trailing lower toward her mons.

"So beautiful," her subjugator murmured. "You are a bedeviling little witch."

His words were nonsensical to Elen, so worked up her body was. She gasped when she felt his mouth kiss her *there,* her eyes flying open and rounding as he ate the piece of tart. She lifted her upper body and supported it with her elbows as she glanced down the length of her and toward the face a scant breath from her intimate place.

Their gazes locked and never wavered. Not even when Lord Hrolf's tongue snaked out and licked at a piece of Elen's flesh she hadn't realized until now was even down there.

She gasped, her already jutting nipples stabbing impossibly farther out. The warlord licked faster, their eyes still locked, as his tongue rapidly darted back and forth on that curious, wondrous piece of flesh.

Elen's head felt too heavy to hold up. She fell onto her back, her eyes closing, on a moan of pleasure. Lord Hrolf growled low in his throat as his mouth latched onto that sensitive, swelling bud and suckled it in the way he'd first suckled her nipples.

"Sweet saints," Elen groaned. "What are you doing to me, Viking?"

He sucked harder and more ferociously, growling into her flesh as her hips instinctively bucked up and her moans grew increasingly loud and wanton. Elen cried out as the bizarre clenching of her belly coiled so tight she was fair certain she was about to explode.

And then she did.

"Ohhh!" Elen screamed, her body involuntarily convulsing for her captor. Blood rushed to her face, heating it, and to her nipples, elongating them. *"Ohhhhhh!"*

It was long moments before Elen could think let alone speak or even move. She'd no notion as to what had just transpired within her, but sensations such as those she'd never before experienced.

Her breathing was labored as her eyes slowly opened and her gaze once more sought out the warlord's. He looked to be having difficulty breathing too, for his warm breath came out in pants against her heated skin.

Oh, aye, Elen resolutely determined. Savages had decidedly embarrassing eating habits. Yet she was unabashedly certain that she could grow accustomed to them.

She swallowed roughly as she stared at her captor, determining that she needed to escape the soonest.

Ivar's cock had never been so hard. He fed his beautiful witch from the palm of his hand. She took nourishment from him like a little baby bird, her lips parting to eat all that he gave her. His muscles had never felt so tense, his breathing never heavy like this. He had seen thirty years, the bed of countless thralls, and been widowed two times, yet not ever had he felt quite like this.

After she'd finished the cheese, bread, and mutton, he took to his back, lying down flat upon the cold ground. He placed a bit of tart on the tip of his cock and held it there before snagging her gaze with his. "Eat," he rasped out, already nigh close to spurting.

Her green eyes widened in the way she had about her that was at once innocent and bedeviling. Much to his approval and astonishment she then, like any obedient bed slave would, followed his command without question.

Elen's pink tongue darted out and took in the piece of tart. She quickly gobbled it down, then obviously recalling what Ivar had done to her, licked at the head of his cock, flicking at the tip with rapid darts. He moaned, his breath stuttering in at the exquisite sensation.

"Does it feel the same way?" she whispered between licks. "The way you made me feel, milord?"

His jaw clenched. "It will when you suck on all of him," he hoarsely informed her.

She hesitated one brief moment, apparently long enough to think his words over. And then finally, blessedly, she wrapped her full rouge lips around the head of his cock and suckled hard.

"That's a good girl," Ivar ground out. One calloused hand found the back of her golden head and prodded her closer. "Suck all of him, Elen. Every inch."

She took more of his cock in. And then more and more and more.

"Ah gods," Ivar groaned, mere moments away from spilling his seed. His new slave learned at an ungodly rate, for in his next heartbeat her mouth, lips, and throat were feverishly working up and down the length of his stiff cock.

The sound of suctioning lips meeting rigid flesh permeated the tent.

He moaned long and loud as he watched her suckle him, her head bobbing up and down at a wicked pace. Ivar's nostrils flared as his body prepared to spurt. Unable to stave off his climax for even another heartbeat, the vein at his neck bulged as he gritted his teeth and came with a bellow.

The milk from his cock must have surprised her, for Elen's bedeviling eyes rounded when his liquid hit the back of her throat. She didn't refuse his seed, though, arousing him impossibly more. She drank all he gave her, every last drop, before she unlatched her swollen lips from around his cock with a popping sound.

His breathing heavy, Ivar stared at his captive for long moments without speaking a word. He briefly considered ordering her to stay the whole of the eve with him, but realized if he did her maidenhead would be severed before the morn.

She was a virgin—he was certain of it. He'd been sure since the moment he got a good look up her tight pussy. He'd never mounted a virgin before, had never possessed a wench no other man had taken to the bedsheets.

And that, Ivar conceded, exhaling slowly, he wanted to savor. No rushing, no quick fuck. He wanted to spend an entire eve glutting himself full of his prize. Loathe as he was to admit it, 'twas more than her maidenhead that aroused him. He coveted it because it belonged to this icy witch in particular.

"You were a very good girl, Elen," Ivar murmured. One hand reached out and brushed a golden curl away from her brow. "Remove yourself from your Master's tent anon lest the need to mate this eve overwhelms me."

Ivar frowned, his gaze tracking her movement. He didn't know whether he should be content or disheartened when his slave did as she was commanded without a word.

Chapter 5

Elen had never been so angry with herself in all her nineteen years. Last eve she was to have escaped. Instead she
had slumbered the sleep of the dead, fair snoring from the
deepness of it. She suspected the spell that had ensorcelled
her body was a consequence of that curious thing Lord
Hrolf had done to her in his tent. He had called her a
witch, yet Elen had since decided the Viking was mayhap a
warlock.

Thankfully, Lothar had slept most of the day and so
hadn't questioned Elen's presence and whether or not she
had tried to escape. This eve she would make Lothar proud.
This eve the saints would smile on her and she would be free.

Her thoughts strayed to her nieces, Lothar's children.
She prayed they fared well under Viking dominion. She

would get to them and help them escape as soon as she possibly could.

Elen's thoughts next turned to Theodrada. She wondered how she was faring. The Viking captors had decided to leave Theodrada in Chippenham to oversee the daily production of the keep. Sobbing, Elen had been forced from the mother of her heart's side. Looking back, she wished she had not cried in front of Theodrada, for in reaction the slave openly and publicly wept—something she'd never before done.

"Please show my mistress mercy!" Theodrada had begged Lord Hrolf, coming down on her knees before him. "I beseech you, milord, to show her mercy!"

Something in the Viking's gaze had gentled, or so Elen had thought. But a blink of an eye later the ruthlessness was back in those black depths as if that moment of rare compassion had never been. She'd hence decided she'd dreamt it.

It didn't matter. Not really. Tender or merciless, Lord Ivar Hrolf was the barbarian who meant to enslave her. The farther they rode from Wessex, the closer his plans came to reality. She had to escape the soonest.

A small moan was issued by Lothar, gaining him Elen's undivided attention. Forgetting for the moment the task of escaping, she placed her brother's head in her lap and comforted him.

"Shhh," she whispered, softly stroking his brow. "All will be well, Lothar." She bent her neck and kissed his forehead. "You will heal and all will be well."

* * *

Ivar couldn't take his eyes off the comely witch. She held a fascination for him he wished she didn't. Elen was a curious creature filled with surprises and contradictions. But that, he conceded, most likely accounted—at least in part—for her allure.

He rode near to the wagon, pretending obliviousness to her presence whilst feeling anything but. Watching Elen with her brother, seeing for himself the tenderness and caring in all that she did and all that she said where Lord Godeuart was concerned—

His jaw clenched as he firmly told himself it didn't matter. Mayhap the witch of Wessex had a few attributes, yet ice still ran through her blood.

Elen was not only a Saxon, but she was also a Godeuart. Her father had been responsible for atrocities against Viking families that could never be let go unpunished. Death, rape, annihilation—all of that and then some. 'Twas said that an apple never falls too far from its tree. In Ivar's experience, that like as not tended to be true.

Mayhap 'twas no falsehood that Norsemen were ruthless, yet still there was a reason to all that they did. Lord Asser of Godeuart, when alive, had no greater purpose behind the atrocities committed by his hand save that he enjoyed the doing of them.

The apple never falls too far from its tree . . .

Ivar's muscles tensed as he spurred his steed into a gal-

lop and away from the witch of Wessex. He would do well
to remember that.

Ivar laid in the tent, unable to sleep. He tossed and turned,
his cock steel-hard with memories of what Elen's naked,
aroused body looked and tasted like.

He wanted to know more. Namely, he wanted to know
what she *felt* like.

He had vowed unto himself that he would not take her
maidenhead until he was back in his stronghold. He didn't
want to take her here, like this, yet 'twas all his lusty mind
could dwell on.

Does she deserve something better for her first mating than
this tent?

His jaw clenched. Nay, she didn't. There was more to
their history together than the slight she'd dealt him atop
the walls, maiming and killing his men.

Elen's hand in marriage had been promised to Ivar. She
was the only daughter of Lord Asser of Godeuart, the man
who had been, before his death, the wealthiest landholder
in the border town of Chippenham. Ivar was the second
eldest son to a Viking jarl with vast holdings in both Jorvik
and the Northlands.

'Twas a good betrothal and one that had been arranged
by their sires in an effort to bring peace between their two
holdings by joining them through marriage. And, eventually, when Elen begat Ivar's sons, through blood as well.

Ivar's sire had believed Asser Godeuart would hold true to his word. The Saxon lord had, after all, turned down the offer to make Elen the third wife of Ivar's elder brother, Amund, whose holdings were superior to Ivar's because Amund was their father's heir.

The terms of the betrothal were such that Asser would accept only an unwed or widowed son of the Viking jarl who had been given a holding of his own, and that Elen would be that son's one and only wife. Such was the way of the Saxon world—one wife to one husband, as the Saxons believed polygamy to be unholy. Ivar's sire had accepted the terms and decreed that Ivar, twice a widower, would take Lady Elen to wife.

Lord Asser of Godeuart had broken his vow. Ivar doubted he'd ever meant to keep it. The Saxon lord had ridden into the Hrolf stronghold in Mercia under a ruse of peace. Rather than delivering Ivar's bride, as expected, he instead held up his sword and laid siege with his accompanying warriors to the Viking fortress.

He didn't succeed. Asser's subterfuge had, inevitably, resulted in his death.

Never would Ivar forget the words that had last bubbled from his mouth as he lay on the ground, a sword through his stomach, blood and saliva gushing from his mouth. "You will never have Elen," Asser had muttered, his eyes maniacal. "She refused the betrothal. My daughter would rather take her own life than bear spawn of the devil with an unholy savage."

Spawn of the devil. Unholy savage. The slights should have burned, but they didn't. The only slight that had vexed Ivar in the least was hearing from Asser's own vile lips that the Saxon's daughter had refused him as a husband.

That was a reaction uncommon amongst wenches where Lord Hrolf was concerned. Ivar was not given to conceit, yet did he realize his position in life, coupled with the strong, dark looks he'd inherited from his Persian mother, made him the sort of potential groom any bride-to-be would covet for her own.

Not Elen. She despised him.

Knowledge of the hatred and disdain she harbored toward him should have kept Ivar's shaft limp. Instead, much to his irritation, his long, thick cock was painfully hard, pre-cum leaking out the head with thoughts of possessing her.

Chapter 6

Elen lay abed the wagon next to her brother. Lothar was fast asleep, the herbs she'd been given leave to feed him making his deep slumber all the deeper. The Viking guards surrounding the wagon were tossing and turning on their sides a bit more than what Elen had a care for. Such was hardly the ideal scenario when a lady needed to escape.

Perhaps I should have snuck herbs in their mead as well . . .

She closed her eyes in sad resignation, the realization that this eve was not ideal for escape like a punch to the belly. She had to get out of here—*had* to. She had vowed as much unto her brother.

What's more, she feared that Lord Hrolf would ask her to dine with him again. The way her body had responded to the giant was beyond humiliating. The last time he had let her go with her maidenhead still intact. What of the next time?

Elen felt as though she was being disloyal to Baron Lenore every time the Viking touched her. Mayhap the Saxon noble was already dead, but until she had confirmed as much, for all intents and purposes she was still to become his betrothed, and eventually his wife. 'Twas likely William would refuse the marriage if he learned of the carnal sensations her captor had forced upon her.

Or of the wanton way Elen's body had responded to the barbarian's touch.

She sighed, forcing thoughts of Ivar Hrolf away. She needed to focus on Baron Lenore, not on the Viking. William was the only man her sire and brother had selected for her to take as a husband. To think on any man but him was blasphemy. And yet, unbidden, her thoughts continually strayed to the giant.

He, her enslaver, had made her feel things in her mind and body that Elen had never before experienced. 'Twas as confounding as it was humiliating.

Closing her eyes, she forced her mind ablank. She needed to sleep. On the morrow, she would require every bit of energy and cunning she could muster. Whether or not the next eve seemed ideal for escape, Elen would attempt to flee regardless.

On the morrow, Elen. One more eve and you will be free . . .
Or dead.

* * *

Deep in slumber's grasp, Elen whimpered a bit as she dreamt she was being touched and fondled by the Viking's demanding, calloused hands. She sighed as he kneaded her breasts and sucked on her jutting nipples.

It felt glorious. Wickedly, wondrously delicious.

"*Mmmm,*" her captor purred from around a stiff nipple. "You are being a good girl for your Master this eve."

Frowning, her eyelashes slowly batted open. Elen tensed up as her conscious mind realized 'twas no dream. Somehow, the Viking had carried her to his tent whilst she slept. He was naked and on top of her now, his muscled body intimately positioned between her splayed thighs. Elen's green dress had been pulled down to her waist, exposing her large breasts to him.

"What are you doing?" she gasped. Her heart rose and fell in her chest as she watched Lord Hrolf greedily suckle at her breasts. Half aroused and half terrified, she didn't know whether to scream for help or moan like a wanton.

The Viking didn't answer her with words, but with deeds. His dark head lifted up and his heavy-lidded gaze drank in the sight of her as he tugged at her dress until it was all the way off.

His breathing deep and heavy, the warlord took to his knees and began to intimately fondle her, touching her where and how he pleased, as much as he pleased. Her nipples, her navel, her mons, the flesh between her legs . . .

Elen's eyes went wide. He was letting her know with nary a word that she was his possession. He would do with her what he would and there was nothing anyone could do to stop him.

Fight him, Elen! Don't let him take you!

One part of her wanted to resist, for she knew that after this eve transpired William Lenore would shun her if she didn't tell her future betrothed a sinful lie and let him believe her to be an untouched virgin. Mayhap the least she could do to assuage her conscience was put up a brave resistance.

But the other part of her, the far more primal piece of her being, wanted the barbarian to have his carnal way with her. Both for reasons of survival and, loathe as she was to admit it, for reasons of immoral desire.

Lord Hrolf made her body and mind feel sensations she hadn't known possible before being captured by him. She was fair tempted to see how far these sensations went, to know all there was to know of being possessed by a man, before she made good on her escape.

Desire won out.

"Will you kiss me like you did before?" Elen breathed, her voice throaty in a way she didn't recognize. She arched her hips, giving him an explicit view of her flesh. "Down there, milord?"

Every muscle in Ivar's body tensed at her lusty words. Ever since the eve their two sires had agreed on a betrothal between them, he had spent countless hours thinking on the things he would do to his beautiful virgin wife when at last she was his.

He had heard the stories of her beauty from those who had ridden to Chippenham, but hadn't known whether or not the tales were true. He had found himself obsessed regardless, eager to see for himself the untouched prize he was to collect from the marriage bargain. Elen hadn't become his in quite the manner Ivar had planned, and yet here she was—naked, untried, and lying submissively before him.

Forgoing words, he answered her with actions. Burying his face in her tight, wet pussy, he all but came from naught but hearing Elen moan. Suckling her little clit in the way he knew she liked best, Ivar groaned against her flesh as her legs shook from around his head.

"Milord," she gasped, grinding her drenched cunt into his face. "I—I'm about to—to . . ."

She didn't know the word for the sensation, mayhap didn't even know what it was. But he knew she wanted it.

Elen came on a loud moan, her entire body shaking as she used her legs to pull his face as deeply into her flesh as she could. His eyes open and peering over her flat belly, he watched her nipples stab up as her head lulled back on her neck.

His breathing labored, Ivar gave her hole one last suck before relinquishing it. The head of his swollen cock found the entrance to her virgin flesh as he palmed both of her large breasts and frenziedly began sucking on her nipples.

Stiff and hard, they were delicious. He wanted to take his time and savor the feel of them in his mouth, but her continuous moans all but sent him over the edge.

"Milord," Elen whispered, her hands buried in his thick, black hair, "*Please*. I want—oh, I—I—this feels so good."

Arching her back, she thrust her chest up higher. It was all Ivar could stand not to plow into her as if she was a well-loved woman, instead of like the untouched wench she was.

Releasing her nipple with a popping sound, his dark head slowly rose until their gazes clashed. Perspiration dotted both of their foreheads, their breathing mutually heavy. "I've been waiting for this moment for years," Ivar rasped.

Elen blinked, but said nothing. She looked confused by his words. He didn't know what to think of that, so he ignored it.

His jaw tight, Ivar rested his weight on his left elbow, using his right hand to perfectly position his cock at her opening. "You are *mine*, Elen," he ground out, pressing the tip in just a bit. "You have always been mine."

Her green eyes widened. "Milord? I don't understand . . ."

His jugular vein bulged, possessiveness engulfing him. On a groan, Ivar seated himself to the hilt, tearing through her maidenhead, branding her as his. She cried out, her eyes squeezing tightly shut.

"It hurts," she whimpered, her eyes flying open as she tried in vain to push him away from her. "I do not desire this anymore. Please, Lord Hrolf—"

"Shhh," Ivar consoled as best he could through a clenched jaw. Ah gods, her cunt was so fucking tight. He felt nigh close to exploding already. 'Twas the middle of winter, yet sweat dripped off of him. "You will feel good in a moment, beautiful Elen."

She gazed up at him with the most innocently frightened expression on her face. It did things to his heart he wished it didn't.

"Lie still," he said thickly, his eyelids as heavy as his breathing. "I promise I will not hurt you."

Ivar began to kiss her, soft, gentle kisses that he knew would arouse her. On her shoulders, on her neck, everywhere that would make her want him again. His muscles were corded, the desire to fuck her hard nigh unto overwhelming, but he didn't move within her, just let her grow accustomed to the feeling of him possessing her.

By the time her body went limp and she began to quietly gasp, Ivar was more than ready to move his throbbing cock in and out of her. He began making love to her, long, slow strokes that were as branding as they were pleasurable.

"Elen," he ground out, "you feel so good. I love how tight and perfect you fit me."

She said nothing to that, but her soft gasps let Ivar know she was enjoying the sensations. He began to move faster, pushing his hard cock in and out of her sticky, glorious flesh.

"Oh God," Elen moaned. "Milord—oh—ohhhh!"

"Do you like this?" Ivar asked thickly, arrogantly, his

nostrils flaring. He sank into her faster, one hand territorially grabbing a fistful of golden curls. "Tell Master how much you like him to be inside you."

"I like it," she gasped. Her lips parted on a groan, her hips rearing up. "I love the way you make me feel."

"Master," he gritted out, fucking her harder. He slammed in and out of her, over and over, again and again. *"Call me Master."*

She refused to speak the word. At least for now, he was beyond caring.

Taking her the way he had oft dreamt of riding her, Ivar ruthlessly pumped in and out of her pussy. He moaned as he fucked her, every stroke more pleasurable than the last. The sound of flesh slapping against flesh heightened his fervor. The tangy scent of combined arousal permeated the tent. He took her harder, faster, deeper, branding her as his. Over and over. Again and again and—

"Ah gods—Elen."

Ivar's entire body stilled atop hers, then convulsed on a roar. He kept up the pace, fucking her hard as he came, letting her tight cunt milk him of all seed. His cock jerked inside her, cum spurting out in a series of gluttonous throbs.

"Elen," he rasped, his heart beating like mad in his chest. He had spent himself so hard he felt nigh ready to collapse. "Elen, thank you."

She stiffened beneath him, causing Ivar to recall their roles here. Master and slave. Conqueror and the conquered. He was not her husband, he was her enemy.

This is what you wanted, Hrolf. Isn't it?

Ivar's grim, dark gaze clashed with a wide green one. She was as surprised by his declaration of gratitude as he was.

Rolling off Elen's body, he took to his side. "Get some sleep, slave," he said gruffly, refusing to look upon her, refusing to deal with anything but the fact that his body coveted hers. "You'll need it."

Elen stared up at the tent, seeing nothing, hearing nothing. She had never been more confused in her life.

The talk of having waited for *years* to be joined with her, had that been naught but an exaggeration of time in a fevered moment of passion? It made no sense. She could conjure up no explanation other than that one. And—

He had *thanked* her. Elen blew out a breath, stunned. The barbarian had actually thanked her for their mating. She had not been expecting such thoughtful words from such a heartless brute.

Is he a brute? He has never harmed you. By the saints, he hasn't even hurt Lothar!

Contradictions. Nothing was black and white anymore.

Elen supposed she should feel guilt for her lack of a maidenhead, but her only sense of shame was born from the fact that she didn't. She had wanted Lord Hrolf to touch her as much as he had wanted to do it. She could deny it, but what was the point? He had captured and enslaved her, wanted her to call him Master, and yet she had still craved his touch.

More contradictions.

The Viking was mayhap sound asleep beside her, but Elen knew slumber would be a hard won boon for herself. She closed her eyes and tried not to think, desperately wanting this eve, and the bizarre emotions and thoughts that had accompanied it, to end.

Chapter 7

"A good bed slave is awake *before* her Master, anticipating his every need."

Elen's eyelids batted in rapid succession as she forced them open. A beeswax candle flickered, drawing her attention. Groggy with sleep, it took her a suspended moment to realize it was still nighttime. "Mayhap 'tis because the saints made me a lady and not a slave," she sniffed. "I will not make for a good bed slave at all."

There was a glint of some unnamed emotion that sparked in his unsmiling eyes. Amusement? Irony? Admiration? She didn't know. He said nothing, only watched her.

She frowned as she sat up. Recalling her nudity, she raised her hands to cover her breasts. Ridiculous, mayhap, considering there was no part of her body the Viking hadn't seen, and yet she did it anyway.

"Do not shield what belongs to me."

"I do not belong to you."

"Oh?" One dark eyebrow quirked. He glanced down at her golden triangle and then back to her face. "Do you not?"

Elen blushed, the reminder of her wanton behavior nigh unto turning her entire body a horrid shade of crimson.

"Lower your hands," he murmured. "I like looking at my slave naked."

She lowered her hands, her blush deepening as she watched him stare his fill at her. His brooding gaze wandered the length of her body, taking in her mons, memorizing the stiff nipples that jutted off soft pink pads. That bedamned knot of tension that had a tendency to coil inside her belly whenever the barbarian coveted her chose that moment to rear its sinful head.

"What do you do to me, Viking?" she whispered. "I do not understand this."

Silence.

Elen glanced up. Their gazes met and locked.

"Touch yourself," Ivar said thickly. "Play with your pretty nipples until your pussy is sopping wet for me."

She hesitated, uncertain what to do.

"Touch them," he murmured, his voice deep and aroused. "Pluck them and pinch them."

Elen slowly ran her hands over her breasts. Her teeth sank into her lower lip as she listened to his breathing grow heavy. Uncertain as to exactly what it was he wanted to see, but encouraged by his lust, she clamped either nipple between her thumbs and forefingers and began to pull at the hard peaks. Immediately, she moaned, the knot in her belly coiling tighter.

"Keep playing with them," he said hoarsely. "Pull them harder."

She did. Elen pinched her nipples tighter, tugging them at the same time. Instinctively, her hips began to move just a little, the arousal she felt in her belly spreading to where he'd impaled her with his rod only a couple of hours hence.

"Please," she whispered, her eyes drifting shut as she massaged her nipples. "This is making me ache, milord."

Ache in a good way. He knew it, and she knew it, too.

"Do you want Master to fuck you?" Ivar murmured.

"Aye," she breathed out. By the saints, she felt nigh unto fevered. Her hips kept up a slow, steady undulation as she pulled at and pinched her nipples. "Please, milord."

Silence.

Elen felt ready to explode, but couldn't quite bring herself to the edge. She needed more. She tweaked her nipples even harder, hoping it would appease him, praying he would show her a bit of mercy and make the knot in her belly come undone.

"Please, milord." Oh God, how she ached! "I need your touch."

"Nay," he said in low tones, making her whimper. "You will play with your nipples until you scream out my name and *beg* for my touch."

Master. She knew precisely what name he meant for her to call him by.

Elen gasped as she played with her nipples, the ache growing worse and more torturous by the second. She squeezed her thighs together, hoping it would assuage the fire, but found that it only made it worse.

The game was over. She had lost.

"Please," Elen pleaded, her voice sounding desperate. "Please touch me, Master." Her eyes flew open and clashed with his. She clamped down on her nipples hard, causing her to gasp. *"I beg you."*

His jaw tightened, his arousal obvious. "That's a very good girl," he murmured. "Now get down on your hands and knees and offer my slave's pussy to me."

Elen all but fell to the ground. Breathing heavily, she took to her hands and knees, her posture imitating a cat. Sweet saints, but she would have meowed had he commanded her to—anything to end the ache.

Calloused fingers dug into the flesh of her hips at the precise moment she was impaled from behind. Elen moaned, the invasion welcomed. She could hear his answering growl, a sound that only further intensified the longing within.

He wasted no time in vanquishing her body, mercilessly slamming his long, thick erection into her with furious strokes. He pounded into her hard—harder—*harder*—causing the knot in her belly to explode.

"Milord—Master!"

Elen groaned as the violent sensation ripped through her womb. He took her impossibly harder, her buttocks instinctively meeting him thrust for thrust. The suctioning sound of their sexes meeting resonated throughout the tent.

"You are all mine," Ivar gritted out from behind her, his fingers digging even farther into her hips. He rode her faster and harder, deeper and more ferociously. *"Only mine."*

He slammed into her flesh once, twice, three times more before a loud growl echoed throughout the tent. Warm seed flooded Elen's insides, snapping her back to reality.

She could be pregnant. Even now, Lord Hrolf's babe could be in her belly.

Collapsing to the ground, Elen's thoughts raced as she panted for air. *What if . . . ?*

Ivar flipped her over, kissing her senseless, and all fears immediately fled—just as they always did in the barbarian's carnal presence. From somewhere in the back of her passion-drunk mind, Elen realized that she had to flee the soonest. The longer she stayed, the harder 'twould be to leave.

In more ways than one.

Getting the captives back to Mercia should have been the priority. Instead, the Vikings made camp for two more days and nights at Ivar's command that he might glut himself full of Elen's body.

Elen.

He couldn't get his fill of her no matter how many times he took her. The innocent way her eyes would round as she found her climax, the sexy look she'd give him from over her shoulder while he rode her from behind, the tight, wet feel of her pussy squeezing around his cock.

And, he thought, blowing out a breath as Elen bounced up and down on top of him, the way her gorgeous tits would jiggle as she rode him.

He loved it all. There was nothing about Elen, sexually or otherwise, that didn't arouse him. She was his possession, mayhap, but she was also his obsession.

This wasn't how Ivar had envisioned keeping Elen. Force hadn't been a part of the betrothal plans. He *could* do the honorable thing and marry her . . .

She refused the betrothal, dunce! Elen may be beautiful, but ice runs through her veins.

Or did it? He no longer knew.

The love Elen harbored for her brother, Lothar, was obvious in its purity. The loyalty she held for her bedamned Chippenham was undeniable. The protectiveness and devotion she had exerted toward Theodrada, her servant, and the moonstruck way she was looking down at Ivar now . . .

You confound me, little girl. I do not know the difference between truth and falsehood anymore.

His nostrils flaring, Ivar reversed their positions. He fucked Elen harder than he'd ever fucked her before, his rage, hatred, love, confusion, and admiration coalescing into a single orgasm. She hugged him tightly to her as he came, further confounding him.

"I wanted everything from you, Elen," Ivar growled, his battle-roughened hands sifting through her hair. "Why didn't you give it to me?"

She searched his eyes, her expression confused. "Milord?"

Milord. She hadn't referred to him as Master since their first morning together and, for reasons unknown, Ivar hadn't pushed her to, either.

"The betrothal," he gritted out, his hands tightening in her golden hair.

She blinked several times in rapid succession. "I—the betrothal?" She frowned, then lifted a hand to his head. "I think you've the fever, milord. Your words are nonsensical."

Ivar didn't have the fever, but neither was he of a mind to play games. She had to know what betrothal he was speaking of. Feigning ignorance of her past deeds made him hurt in a way he never had before.

"Leave my tent," Ivar said coldly, rolling off her, giving her his back.

"Milord?" He heard her sit up.

On the morrow they could and would discuss this once and for all. For now, all he wanted was to be alone with his tumultuous thoughts. Truly, he no longer recognized left from right, up from down.

"You may sleep with your brother in the wagon to-night. Go to him, Elen."

He could hear her hesitation. And then, for the second time in Ivar's life, he didn't know whether he should be content or disheartened when Elen did as she was commanded without a word.

Chapter 8

Feigning a deep, measured sleep, Elen waited for what felt to be days for Ivar and his men to fall, one by one, into slumber. Her heart was beating so fast and mightily she could scarce hear anything but its steady pounding.

Guilt consumed her. For one, were she to find William Lenore, she would have to confess her lack of a maidenhead to him prior to any betrothal taking place. He could very well refuse to marry her altogether.

But that wasn't the worst. To Elen's way of thinking, the ugliest sin she had committed was in no longer caring if Baron Lenore wanted her or not.

Elen realized that a part of her had changed, matured, those two eves in the tent with Lord Hrolf. That part of her, for better or for worse, would always belong to Ivar.

He wanted everything from her, but she could only give him that part. Mayhap had he not wished to keep her as a slave.

She shook the thought away. "Mayhap" meant naught. The Viking *did* wish to enslave her, no "mayhap" about it.

Let him go, Elen. He wanted you to leave his tent. Let him go.

She wondered if that was the real reason behind her choosing this eve in particular to finally make good on her vow to Lothar. Were she honest with herself, Ivar had all but slept like the dead the past two nights. Not once had she thought to escape him, let alone tried. But this eve—

Her feelings were smarting. Lord Hrolf had injured her heart in a way she hadn't known the Viking could until it had happened.

Taking a deep breath, she quietly sucked in a soothing tug of wintry air and forced herself to expel all thoughts of Ivar from her mind. She had to calm down. Elen realized that if she wished to escape she would need her wits—and hearing—about her.

They are asleep. The Vikings are all deep within slumber's grasp.

'Twas now or 'twas never.

Briefly closing her eyes, Elen offered up a quick prayer to the saints, silently begging for divine intervention, for aid from God that she might find her way back to Wessex and onward to King Alfred.

Her eyes flew open. She assessed once again that the Vikings were all aslumber.

Oh, my beloved brother, how I despise leaving you here to suffer at the merciless hands of Ivar's men!

Elen hesitated for a brief moment as she glanced down at Lothar, her heart in her eyes. But this, she realized, was what her brother wanted. Mayhap all of Wessex depended upon her cunning. She *had* to escape.

Pausing long enough to gently kiss Lothar atop the head, Elen brushed back a stray blond curl from his brow, smiled down into his sleeping face, and quietly made her way from off the wagon. Her knees wobbled and her heart took to pounding again as she inched her way past more sleeping Viking warriors than she cared to contemplate. If they caught her—

Her gaze flicked to the tent where Lord Hrolf was sleeping. 'Twas the last barrier between her and the shelter of the forest.

Memories assaulted her. Recollections of his touch, his kiss, the way he made love to her womanhood with his mouth. The way his swollen manpart sank inside her, filling her up, making her feel secure and wanted.

Cease this, Elen! Ivar does not love you. You are but chattel to him!

Elen felt nigh close to swooning so furious was the pounding of blood in her heart. Beads of sweat caused her forehead to glisten. Her breathing grew heavier than what was healthy. Her breasts heaved up and down from beneath the green dress and wool blankets she hadn't donned for two days.

Stay slow and stay steady. You can do this. You are nigh into the woods already. You must *leave.*

Elen found her resolve and steadied her heartbeat once more. Quietly, oh so quietly, she crept soft-footedly past the slumbering warlord's tent and into the anonymity of the surrounding forest. She continued inching into the depths of the dark woodlands for what felt to be hours, but was mayhap only thirty minutes, afraid to so much as rustle a leaf for fear Ivar's savages would awaken. As soon as the makeshift camp was well out of earshot, she began to run.

The bittersweet feel of victory and sadness simultaneously surged through Elen, pounded in her veins. She ran and ran, faster and faster, her arms furiously pumping back and forth, her heart drumming against her chest. *I did it! I escaped!* She had not yet made it to Wessex, mayhap, yet she had escaped.

Lady Elen of Godeuart had vowed unto herself that she would be no man's slave. A part of her would always long for his touch, would mayhap even miss those two eves in the tent, but 'twas a pledge she intended to keep.

Goodbye, Ivar. I shall miss you more than you will ever realize. If only the fates had brought us together under different circumstances. . . .

Elen fervently reminded herself there was no time for "if onlys." There was only time to keep her pledge to Lothar.

*   *   *

Ivar awoke to the sound of his men's angered shouts. He quickly blinked away the last remnants of sleep and ran a hand over his eyes before exiting the tent. Pulling on his brais, he stood up and speedily made his way toward the wagon where Olaf was currently manhandling the injured Lord Godeuart.

Olaf was fiercely angry, his face red, the veins in his biceps bulging as he picked the Saxon up by the scruff of the neck. Spittle from words that were barely audible at such a distance spattered from his mouth and against the felled noble's face.

Ivar frowned. "What goes on here?" he barked in their common tongue. "Olaf!" he shouted, nearing the wagon. "What goes on here?"

Olaf let go of the dangling Lord Godeuart, a groan issuing from the injured man as he fell back against the wagon. Ivar's most trusted man turned to face him then. His breathing was labored, his face a mask of unadulterated fury.

"She is gone," Olaf ground out. Ivar stilled. "The wench escaped whilst we slumbered, milord."

Ivar was so shocked it took him a moment for Olaf's words to sink in. *Escaped? Elen had escaped?*

And then came the anger—fury—at the knowledge he had been bested not once, but twice, by the icily beautiful witch of Wessex. Oh, aye, she was cunning! Feigning at submissiveness and even the beginnings of a love whilst plotting his humiliation all the while. Ivar's jaw clenched.

You told her to leave your tent, idiot. Did you not bark at her to remove herself from your presence?

Elen had made him *feel.* Something he hadn't wanted to do. Not with her. Not with Asser Godeuart's daughter. And yet—

"Where is she?" Ivar bellowed, jumping in the wagon with four long strides. His nostrils flared and his teeth gritted as he pulled Lord Godeuart's hair back and forced him to look up. The muscles around the gold clasp that encircled Ivar's arm bulged in his rage. "Where," he bit out, "is she?"

The Saxon's smile was weak but powerfully irritating. "Long gone from here," Lothar Godeuart rasped. "Do with me what you will. My sister is free."

For all certainty, Ivar was sorely of a mind to do with him what he would, yet he stayed his hand from causing the Saxon further injury. He didn't know the why of it, but deeply suspected 'twas because he knew in his heart Elen would never forgive him did her brother die at his hands.

It irritated him all the more that he should care. He was a warrior, for the love of the gods! Warriors did what they did without thoughts of how 'twould cause hurt to a wench's heart. Especially a wench possessed of a heart as icy and cold as Elen's.

How could you leave me? How! I was growing to love you. Bedamn you!

"Where," Ivar ground out, his teeth gnashing together, "is my thrall?" He tightened his hold on Lothar's neck, causing the Saxon lord to bellow in pain. "Speak!"

"I—I don't know," Lothar said on a gasp. Ivar shook him. "I know naught!"

"He'll know something before I'm through with him!" Olaf spat.

"Wessex," Lothar weakly admitted. He would say no more than what was obvious. " 'Tis all I know."

Ivar suspected he knew more, yet did he also realize this particular Godeuart would die before giving up his sister's intended whereabouts. On one level, he respected him for it—'twas more nobility than Lothar's sire had ever shown—but on another and far more primal level the Saxon's loyalty was deeply frustrating.

Lord Hrolf held up a palm when Olaf looked ready to tear into the Godeuart heir. "Acquire as much information as you can from the other of our captives. Do it now!" Ivar's jaw clenched impossibly tighter. "The wench mayhap has a five-hour head start, yet she is on foot. We are not."

Olaf nodded, seeing the wisdom in his argument. Pausing but long enough to throw a scowl Lothar's way, he stormed from the wagon and to the other side of camp where the ten slaves they'd brought with them had been corralled.

Ivar's black gaze clashed with Lothar's blue one. "I will find her," Ivar growled, earning him a frown. " 'Tis doubtful your slaves—*my* new slaves," he said pointedly, "will share in your silence."

Lothar's eyes narrowed. Ivar sighed, shook his head, and walked away.

It took even less time than Lord Hrolf had surmised. Where Elen's brother felt and displayed a loyalty toward his sister that cut bone-deep, the former Godeuart thralls felt loyalty up until the point where 'twas their own bones that would be cut. Such was the way of slaves and was to be expected. In the end, the most valuable lead came from the mouth of a babe, a six-year-old girl who was a veritable fountain of information without even realizing it.

"Do you know where she might have gone?" Ivar murmured, squatting down on his thighs that they might be the same height. Elen was not so lack-witted as to return to Chippenham. Nay. If there was one thing the witch of Wessex was not, 'twas lacking in smarts. "Was she friendly with any Saxon ladies perchance? Or a nobleman mayhap?"

The little girl nodded. "Aye, Master."

"Go on," he said softly.

"Um . . . well . . . I forget his name, milord."

Ivar stilled. *His* name? He forced a small, gentle smile to his lips whilst his gut clenched with hot jealousy. He shouldn't care—he knew that. Yet he did. Possessing Elen's body, branding her with his seed, had changed everything. "Mayhap if you think real hard 'twill come to you, wee one."

The little girl squeezed her eyes tightly shut, her concentration obvious. Ivar's blood churned and boiled on the inside whilst on the outside he exhibited a patience he felt far from feeling.

"Baron Lenore," the little girl squeaked. Her eyes flew open. She smiled at him, her toothless grin making him smile back. "Baron William Lenore was to be betrothed to milady."

Jealousy. There it was again. Hot and all-consuming. It caused his heart to relentlessly pound and every muscle in his body to clench and cord. It wasn't to this William Lenore Elen was to have been betrothed—'twas to Ivar.

Ivar inclined his head. "Seflik," he murmured to a nearby warrior, "take this girl to the tent and let her choose a tart or two." He patted the child-slave on the head before she skipped away.

Standing up, he turned to Olaf. "Ready our mounts." His jugular vein bulged. "We will find this William Lenore the soonest."

Chapter 9

Two weeks later

Battling and bloodshed had broken out everywhere. 'Twas becoming harder and harder to find a village the barbarians had not yet laid siege to within Wessex. Chippenham, she'd quickly discovered, had already surrendered—not just the conquered Godeuart stronghold, but the whole of the village. Such knowledge had dampened her already downcast spirits, yet she continued onward, deeper into Wessex, her promise to Lothar firmly etched in her mind and heart.

Making her mission more daunting still, Elen was forced to keep to the woodlands more oft than not for fear of being discovered. A lady traveling without escort *before* the Vikings had overthrown parts of Wessex had been naught but trouble. But now? The fear of rape and enslavement made an already worrisome situation that much more terrifying.

Elen's saving grace as it were had come in the form of a young boy, a thief of horses! Exhausted from two grueling days of traveling on foot, she had gladly exchanged the single jade brooch she'd had in her possession for a healthy steed capable of taking her as deep into Wessex as she needed to venture. She'd named the horse Louis, in deference to the fourteen-year-old brother she'd lost at Viking hands.

The days were long and tiring, the nights cold and lonely. In the eves when Elen would make camp, her thoughts oft drifted back to her brother, Lothar. And, as much as she wished it otherwise, to the bedamned barbarian who'd captured the both of them.

She wondered if her brother fared well, but realized what a bloodthirsty lot warring men were—Vikings and Saxons alike. Even her sire, as loathe as she was to admit it, had seemed at times rather obsessed with battling.

Surely her Viking captor was no different. Mayhap worse even than Elen's sire had been. Such didn't bode well for Lothar. He was a nobleman within the very realm the Vikings sought to hold all dominion over.

King Alfred had offered the savages much Danegeld to leave, to return to the Viking stronghold of Mercia and forsake Wessex. Their jarls—their kings—had accepted. They had lied. Danish Mercia was indisputably theirs, but 'twas now Saxon Wessex their heathen hearts were set on acquiring.

Elen was weary of all of them, Saxon and Viking. She

had long since grown tired of the battling, bloodshed, and politics, yet at this moment she felt obligated to aid her countrymen in whatever way she could. Or, mayhap more to the point, she felt a sense of duty to keep the vow she'd made to Lothar.

Leastways, 'twas not about war and politics to Elen. 'Twas about the lesser of two evils. Did the Vikings overthrow King Alfred, every Saxon lady might very well be subjected to slavery. And, mayhap just as sadly, the Saxon way of life would die out, their entire culture reduced to naught but ashes and memories in the name of heathen gods and the polygamous ways of the terrible Northmen.

And, of course, there was her vow to her beloved brother, Lothar, which needed to be kept. 'Twas his dying wish that she find William Lenore, King Alfred, or preferably both.

Sighing, Elen snuggled into the wool blankets she'd carried with her since her escape and lay down next to the flickering embers of the warm makeshift fire she'd crafted. Her jade-green eyes stared into the flames as if searching them, though her mind was a blank slate of stone.

Slowly, almost druggedly, her eyelids batted and closed. She fell into a deep, restful sleep, the hope that on the morrow she would find aid, her last coherent thought.

That eve, like every eve, 'twas not King Alfred or Baron William Lenore who called to Elen in her dreams. 'Twas the ruggedly dangerous yet beautifully masculine face of the barbarian who beckoned to her.

And memories of the wicked things he'd done to her body those nights in his tent.

It seemed a lifetime ago. Had the barbarian not meant to enslave her, her slumber-fevered mind wondered how much of a fight she'd have put up at being his.

A sennight quickly, frustratingly, turned into a fortnight. Had the escaped wench in question been any but Elen, he'd have given up his hunt long ago—if indeed he would have even bothered with one in the first. But Elen . . .

She was his. She had always been his. She had been promised to him five years ago, when she had seen but fourteen years.

"Milord!"

Ivar blinked, his thoughts returning to the present. He craned his neck, his dark eyes watching Olaf stampede toward him. He was atop his warhorse, riding from out of the woodlands and into the makeshift camp they'd set up a few hours outside Chippenham.

Olaf had gone off scouting with two other of the Hrolf warriors. Ivar prayed to the gods that this time his man had found some useful information. Judging from the arrogant look on Olaf's face, he suspected he had. Ivar found his hopes rising for the first time in days. "Aye?"

"She headed north!" Olaf shouted to be heard over the sound of clapping hooves. He slowed his gait as he approached Ivar. "Toward Ashdown."

Ivar's gut clenched. "You are certain?"

"Aye," Olaf panted. He was breathing heavily, his speed at returning obvious despite the cold weather slashing him in the face. "I finally got that old Celtic slave to talk."

"Theodrada?"

"Aye."

Ivar's heartbeat sped up, though his features were schooled. "And . . . ?"

"William Lenore's stronghold is in Ashdown. The old slave believes 'tis the only logical place to hunt for her."

Ivar ran the bit of information through his mind. "That particular thrall seems more loyal than most. How do you know Theodrada isn't just trying to throw us off her scent?"

"I don't."

Ivar narrowed his eyes.

"But . . ."

"Aye?"

Olaf scratched his yellow beard. "I can't explain it," he muttered, frowning. "Just a feeling."

Ivar quirked an eyebrow.

" 'Tis just something there in the old slave's eyes. A fear. Almost as though she'd rather we recapture Elen than for the wench to find Baron Lenore."

Ivar frowned. 'Twas odd. Too odd that one so loyal as Theodrada would wish enslavement upon Elen rather than seeing her safely wed to this William. And yet did Olaf's instincts rarely run afoul.

"And there's more," Olaf grumbled. At Ivar's answering

grunt, he sighed. "The old slave claims Elen knew naught of any betrothal between you and her."

Ivar stilled.

"In fact, she claims 'twas the first she'd heard tell of such an arrangement. She doubts even Elen's brother, Lothar, knew of it."

Ivar's gut clenched hotly. His pulse picked up in tempo. "Do you believe her?" he rasped. He blinked, clearing his throat, not having a care for the hint of vulnerability he'd heard in his voice. "Do you believe her?" he asked louder, harsher.

"I do," Olaf asserted. He searched his face. "Her expression was convincingly dumbfounded, milord."

Ivar blew out a breath. If what Theodrada had said could be believed, then he was an even bigger fool than first he'd thought. He'd held Elen responsible for treacherous acts she hadn't known about, let alone committed.

He wished Asser was alive. Namely so he could be killed again.

"Milord?" a young warrior asked. "Do we ride?"

Ivar ran a punishing hand through his night-black hair as he absently glanced at the young Viking. They could continue to ride south where they believed King Alfred to be in hiding. They could head north on Olaf's hunch that the old slave had spoken the truth to him. Or they could sit here at camp and do naught.

In that moment, Ivar knew with all certainty there was nothing he wouldn't do, no lead too farfetched that he wouldn't act upon it, to get his witch back. He wanted her, was obsessed with her.

Elen haunted his dreams in a way no wench ever had before. 'Twas not her beauty, though surely that made the pot sweeter. It wasn't even the broken betrothal, a slight from Asser he doubted he could ever let go of. 'Twas a connection, and one he knew not how to explain. Not even to himself.

"We ride," Ivar decided. He slanted a look at Olaf. Territorial feelings toward Elen coursed through his blood, inducing his muscles to clench. "North. To Ashdown."

Chapter 10

Ashdown, one week later

Baron William Lenore wasn't dead. She'd yet to see him, but it had been confirmed for Elen by William's slaves that he was safely in hiding with King Alfred.

Five days ago, she had sent the only Saxon soldier who had been made privy to his lord's whereabouts with an urgent missive informing William and Alfred of what she knew and of the fact that she was currently at Ashdown. She doubted the majority of her missive would come as a surprise. Not now. Not when all of Wessex lay under siege.

Mayhap the only part of Elen's message that would come as a shock at all was learning that she had escaped from her Viking captors. And that, to the best of her knowledge, Lothar was still alive—most likely to be held for ransom.

She had begged the king to intercede on Lothar's behalf, though she doubted anything would come of her pleading. The king had other things to worry over—like his own backside.

And the fact that all of Wessex looked close to falling.

Elen slowly, aimlessly, strolled down a long corridor within the Lenore stronghold that led toward the dining hall. Ashdown had yet to fall. Then again, Ashdown had yet to be raided! She wondered how long it would take before a Viking army swept into the village and conquered the keep for their own.

Does it matter?

Coming to a halt before a large, well-polished silver plate, Elen sighed as she halfheartedly inspected her dress before the mirror. She looked like the restored Lady Elen of Godeaurt wearing an expensive, if borrowed, burgundy woolen dress.

A gold braided rope knotted around the swell of her belly and drooped directly above her mons. Her long, blonde curls once again cascaded down her back to her bum, a wreath of golden braids encircling the top of her head.

Elen *looked* like her former self. She just didn't *feel* like her.

'Twas difficult at best and impossible at worst to care about much of anything when those she loved were either dead or captured. Theodrada—a slave mayhap, yet still the mother of her heart—imprisoned within the walls of Chippenham alongside her nieces. Lothar—her beloved brother and the true heir of Chippenham—enslaved, if not dead, at only the saints knew where within enemy territory. The barbarian!

Elen sighed. She had escaped from Lord Ivar Hrolf three weeks hence, yet the image of him was permanently branded in her mind. For better or for worse, she would never forget him. Though her conqueror, he was a solid presence in an uncertain world, the sort of larger than life warrior her papa would have wanted her to have as a husband. And the way Lord Hrolf had created magic in her body—

'Twas a shame he had meant to enslave her.

"Milady!"

Elen blinked. She whirled around to face the voice that had excitedly called out to her. 'Twas a slave-girl, a beauty named Arda who had mayhap seen eighteen years. She must have been a disobedient slave, for the girl's legs were fair covered with whipping scars. "Aye? What is it?"

Arda was beaming from head to toe. "The Master returns! He returns with the king!"

The last declaration got Elen's heart to rapidly beating. It pounded against her chest, inducing her breathing to hitch. "You are certain?" she murmured.

"Aye, milady! Arnell has returned and brought word! They shall be here in two days' ride!"

Arnell was the Saxon soldier Elen had sent to William and Alfred with her missive. The Saxon king's hiding place must not have been too far off since he had returned intact so quickly.

Elen's smile came slowly. Mayhap the king meant to take back Chippenham and all of Wessex. Mayhap he would even pay Danegeld to the Vikings that Lothar could return home! The possibilities made her mind swoon with giddy happiness.

If she couldn't have all that her heart desired, like a certain Viking, then she could at least have freedom. And, most importantly, Lothar.

"Then we shall make certain they return to a feast! Come!" Elen laughed, picking up the hem of her skirts to run. "Let us tell cook to begin preparing food immediately!"

Elen blew out the beeswax candle setting on the stand next to her bed. She sighed as she lay down.

'Twas not the day she had been hoping for. The king had not accompanied William to Ashdown as expected, so beseeching him for intervention on behalf of Lothar was not possible.

Baron Lenore was not what Elen had been expecting, either. Indeed, were she honest with herself, the moment she first clapped eyes on him her heart had fallen with a certain sense of disappointment.

She had expected a strong warlord like her brother, Lothar. Or like Lord Ivar Hrolf: muscular, deadly, powerful, ruthless. But a slight, pale, bejeweled weakling who looked as if he'd never held a sword in his life, not to mention *used* one? How could this man protect his own keep let alone help her reclaim Chippenham?

Nevertheless, Elen understood duty. Lothar had wished to betroth her to Baron Lenore. There had to have been a reason. Lothar *always* had a reason. So William was something of a weakling—what of it? His holdings were vast, which in turn meant his warriors were aplenty. Knowing her brother as well as she did, she realized that her future betrothed's holdings had to have been the draw Lothar saw coming from a union between the deuce of them.

A knock at the door startled her. Naked in her bed, Elen pulled the warm animal skins above her breasts and sat up. Who on earth would come calling so late in the eve?

She trembled as she wondered if Ashdown was currently under siege. "Aye?" She half expected to see her former captor come stalking into the chamber! "Who's there?" she hesitantly inquired, wetting her lips. She couldn't begin to imagine what sorts of hell there would be to pay if *he* caught her. The mere thought got her pulse to racing.

"Elen," a male voice whispered.

It didn't sound like the barbarian. She blew out a breath—from relief, disappointment, or both? She couldn't say.

She stilled. If it wasn't her former captor come to vanquish her, then what man would dare come into a lady's bedchamber in the middle of the night? 'Twas indecent. The saints knew nobody wore clothing abed!

Her question was answered when the wooden door opened and the beeswax candle she'd just extinguished was rekindled. And then another candle. And another.

"Baron Lenore," Elen breathed out, her green eyes round. The strong scent of ale and vomit wafted down from his mouth and into her nostrils. "What are you doing here?"

Apprehension made her heart pound. Whatever the reason William Lenore had for entering her bedchamber unannounced and uninvited, she realized 'twould be no good coming from it. His eyes were bloodshot, his nose running. He was so intoxicated that he could barely stand on his two twiggy legs.

"Elen," he said again, his words slurring together, "I have waited so long for you . . ." He made a motion toward the animal hides. Instinctively, she slapped his bejeweled hand away and held tighter to the skins protecting her naked body from his covetous view.

"William!" she chastised, keeping her voice as low as possible that others in the keep wouldn't hear. *What in the name of the saints is he about?*

She had done all she could to come to him clean, untouched. She had failed, but she had tried. Now he thought to manhandle her prior to their betrothal—let alone their wedding night?

Anger consumed her. Elen was tempted to confront him with the truth of those two eves she'd spent abed with the Viking that William might run off in disgust, but she held her tongue. For now.

"You are drunk," Elen said with a calmness she was far from feeling. "Let us forget this incident ever occurred. Now please, remove yourself from my bedchamber anon."

He paid her no heed. Elen watched in horror as he stumbled toward the bed, and on top of her. She fought back like a wildcat.

"Now, now," William gritted out, clasping her hands together over her head and under one of his. He used his free hand to paw at the animal hides. "We are to be wed, beautiful Elen. No need to be shy."

Tears stung the backs of her eyes. Never had she felt more frightened or humiliated. Even her Viking captor had not treated her thusly. He had been gentle, if demanding, with her.

"Cease this at once!" she cried out, pain lancing through her when he grabbed one of her breasts and began pinching the nipple in a harsh manner. She fought to loose herself from his hold.

The slight man was stronger than he looked. Stronger, leastways, than Elen.

"Baron Lenore!" she pleaded. "I beg of you not to defile me!"

"Defile you?" he raged, his nostrils flaring. He slapped her across the face, inducing her head to swoon. "You should feel grateful a man of my standing is willing to take the lowly heiress of Chippenham to wife!"

That got her goat. Her jaw tightened. "*You* are the one who should be grateful that the *lowly* Chippenham heiress consented to take such a boarish pig as a husband!"

This was all wrong! How could Lothar ever choose such a loathsome creature for her? She wondered if he'd even made the man's acquaintance or if her brother had simply followed their sire's last wish. "Unhand me! *Now!*"

Fighting back only served to heighten his arousal. He slapped her again, this time so hard she felt the inside of her cheek rip against her teeth. Her head lulled back against the bed, momentarily dazed.

"Stop," she gasped. "Please . . ."

He released her long enough to stand up and drunkenly remove his clothes. Elen felt sick as she watched his small penis spring free and erect. 'Twas not at all like the Viking's. The baron's manpart oozed pus from sores and was possessed of warts.

Lothar, forgive me, but for the first time in my life I choose to defy you.

Elen's head was hurting from the slaps she'd been dealt, but she paid the pain no heed. Picking up the brass holder the beeswax candle sat in, she held it before her like a talisman. "Be gone!" she warned, her heart pounding in her chest. "I will use this if you force me to!"

He bellowed with laughter, then lunged. She threw the brass holder at him with every bit of strength she could muster.

Her face paled as the candleholder struck him square in

the forehead. Blood trickled down from the wound as his eyes rolled back into his head and he fell to the floor.

I'm a murderess! Oh dear God, I didn't mean to!

A groaning sound issued from William's throat. Her eyes widened. He wasn't dead. A flicker of relief passed through her, lasting only until she realized that if he woke up and could get to her, she would suffer a worse beating than those two slaps to the face.

Still naked, her heart racing so fast she feared a fainting spell, she shuffled off the bed. Elen grabbed the burgundy dress, her boots, and her cape, but didn't waste time putting them on. She could do that later—

In the woods with no threats looming near.

Chapter 11

Ivar's scouts knew that Elen was within the bedamned keep's gates. Some would think a warrior crazy for laying siege to a stronghold he didn't even want in the name of recapturing a single wench within it. But if that's what it took to reclaim what belonged to him, then so be it.

"Ashdown isn't nearly as fortified as Chippenham," Olaf muttered beside him. "Child's play."

Ivar nodded, but said nothing. 'Twas his thought as well. "Ready the men. We attack at my signal."

Olaf was about to carry through on the warlord's orders when a curious sight reached his eyes. "What in the gods?"

Ivar followed his line of vision. He squinted, barely making out what looked to be boots, then a burgundy dress, and then a cape being thrown over the wooden gate that fortified Ashdown. His forehead wrinkled as he looked to Olaf then back to the peculiar scene. He drew his mount in a little closer, careful not to leave the shield of the forest.

Lord Hrolf's dark eyes widened as he watched an all too familiar face peek up over the gate, and then, grunting something or another about "bedamned splinters," went tumbling over the side of it, long golden curls and all.

She was naked. His jaw dropped.

Shock swiftly coalesced into jealousy, anger, and worry. "Isn't that . . . ?"

"Aye," Ivar barked out to Olaf.

"Holy Odin," Olaf muttered.

Twenty Viking warriors sat atop their warhorses and watched from the trees as a naked, busty Saxon lady picked up her clothing and ran straight toward their position without realizing who she was about to run into.

Her large breasts bobbed up and down as she ran. It infuriated Ivar that his men were staring at her body openmouthed, eyes glazed over. His jaw tightened.

"Show respect," Ivar hissed.

Olaf blinked. "To a *slave*?" He raised an eyebrow. "I thought that's all she was to you." His eyes twinkled.

Ivar's nostrils flared. He said nothing to that, just looked back to Elen and waited for her to reach the forest. They would envelop her as soon as she entered it.

"At least she's making her recapture easy on us, milord," Olaf whispered.

Ivar snorted at that, then waited in silence. Every muscle in his body tensed as he prepared to seize her. The waiting was nigh unto killing him. Elen wasn't that far away, yet she'd stumbled twice already, thereby slowing her pace down.

That wasn't like her. He frowned, wondering why she appeared too dazed to walk, let alone run.

Apparently cold, Elen stopped long enough to quickly don the burgundy dress. She didn't bother with the boots and cloak, just kept them under an arm as she stumbled toward the forest.

At last she was nearing their position. His gut clenched, adrenaline coursing through him. She entered their lair gasping for breath, sounding as bad as her walking looked. Elen appeared—

Crazed. As though her mind had been split asunder.

Ivar gave the signal and Elen was quickly enveloped by twenty Viking warriors. Much to the raiding party's surprise, she didn't attempt to scream. She didn't even look overly horrified at the knowledge she'd been recaptured.

"Oh praise the saints," Elen muttered, her breathing harsh. She turned to Ivar. "I never thought you'd get here."

His eyebrows shot up.

"My brother," she panted, "he is still alive?"

"Aye," Olaf interrupted, his expression looking as stupefied as Ivar felt to be.

Elen nodded. "Good." She began walking again, farther into the forest, twenty Viking warriors following dumbly behind her. "Because I wish to kill him myself."

BARBARIAN

* * *

Elen stumbled as she walked, realizing Ivar probably thought she'd gone daft. Mayhap she had. There was, after all, only so much a lady could endure.

Bloodshed. Battles. The loss of her father and younger brother. Being reduced from a lady to a bed slave. Escape. Near rape. The realization that she'd fare better as Lord Hrolf's slave than as Baron Lenore's wife. Becoming an almost murderess. Scratching up her legs and repeatedly hitting her head on tree branches as she'd climbed up through them, naked, to reach the gate.

Aye, she had mayhap gone daft. What's more, she no longer cared. She would kill Lothar for choosing Baron Lenore to be her husband and that was that.

"Elen!"

'Twas the third time Lord Hrolf had called out to her thusly. Each time the summons grew louder, more insistent. A part of her mind understood this, but the overriding part of it paid him no heed.

"Elen!" He grabbed her by the shoulders and whirled her around to face him. His fingers sunk into the flesh of her arms.

"Elen? Speak to me." His dark eyes roamed over her features, noting the marks William's slaps had left behind on her face.

Her mouth worked up and down. She tried to talk, but

the words simply wouldn't come. She needed sleep. She needed Chippenham. She needed to go back to all that was normal.

"Elen," he said in a low tone that sounded too gentle to come from him, "please speak to me."

"I won't marry him," Elen finally managed, her eyes unblinking. "Not now and not ever. Kill me if you must, send me to the nunnery, or enslave me again. I care not which. I would sooner burn in hell with the devil himself than become William Lenore's wife."

Ivar motioned for his men to keep back. At last he was getting somewhere with her and he didn't want their presence to ruin that. The gods' truth, he'd been worried she'd never come back down. Sanity was slowly returning to her eyes after an hour of walking.

Mounting his steed, Ivar held out a hand, motioning for Elen to come to him. She hesitated but a moment before permitting him to hoist her up onto the warhorse.

For fifteen minutes they rode at a brisk pace until at last they were at the makeshift camp he and his men had erected. Dismounting, he held out his arms and waited for Elen to fall into them.

"I would never send you back to William Lenore," Ivar murmured, reassuring her. "Nor would I send such a passionate woman as yourself to a nunnery."

She blinked. Her head snapped up. "Th–Then you will enslave me again?"

His eyes searched her face. He wanted to question her about the broken betrothal, to know if she was truly the innocent he hoped her to be, but he sensed that she could endure no more this eve.

"Nay. I will not enslave you."

Elen stilled. "I do not understand."

"I love you, Lady Elen of Godeuart." Ivar's heart began to race as he watched her beautiful eyes round in that bedeviling innocent way they had about them. "I love you and I mean to marry you."

Silence ensued. For a moment Ivar wondered if he'd just made a fool of himself yet again. But then Elen was in his embrace, her arms wrapped tightly around his middle.

"I—I love you, too," Elen gasped, squeezing him so hard he had to smile. "By the saints but I've missed you!"

Within moments they were inside Ivar's tent, clawing at each other's clothing and falling to the ground to make love. As he sank inside her, groaning from the exquisite feel of her tight pussy enveloping his cock, Ivar realized that it didn't matter if Elen had broken their betrothal or not. She was his now—his always. The rest didn't signify.

"I've missed you, too, Elen," he rasped, sinking farther into her welcoming, warm flesh. "You will always be mine."

Epilogue

Jorvik, two years later

It had been a long, hard road to travel, but finally all was as it should be. The Saxon king and the Viking jarls had made peace, Chippenham had been returned to Lord Lothar of Godeuart, Theodrada now lived in Jorvik with her mistress, and Elen was happily wed. In a fortnight, the Hrolfs would celebrate two years of marriage. In a few months, Elen would give birth to their second child.

Out of all the happiness Elen had found over the course of the past two years, 'twas but one thorn in her side that she suspected would take a long time to heal—finding out her sire was not the man she had believed him to be. Learning of her broken betrothal to Ivar had felt like a slap to the face. Discovering that her sire had died for laying siege on the Hrolf stronghold rather than delivering her as a promised bride had both embarrassed and shaken her.

Lothar, too, had been stunned. In fact, her brother had not believed Ivar when first he had told him. It had taken him many months to come to terms with all the Viking admitted to him in confidence. In the end, Lothar's pride had relented and he had accepted the fact that there was a side to his and Elen's sire neither of them had been made privy to.

The relationship between Ivar and Lothar was still strained, but progressing. In the beginning, after his release from captivity, Elen's brother had refused to accept a marriage between them—until he'd learned of his sister's pregnancy. In truth, Elen realized that Ivar would have married her regardless of her brother's blessing, yet was she glad that Lothar had granted it, begrudgingly or no.

Smiling down at her sleeping two-year-old son, Eirik, Elen gently removed herself from the bed, then walked to the balcony of her bedchamber. Serfs worked below, toiling in the crisp, wintry air. A ways down the courtyard, Olaf shouted out commands to warriors, teaching them the battling ways of their race.

Breathing in deeply, she sucked in the refreshing air, enjoying her new life in Jorvik far more than she ever had in Chippenham. From countless shopping stalls to rich foods bartered for at market, the city was vibrant with life. Her ancestral country home would always hold a special place in her heart, but naught could compare to the home she'd made with Ivar—the home of her heart.

"What are you thinking about, my love?"

Elen jumped at the sound of her husband's voice. She

hadn't expected him to return from market so soon. He and five Vikings had taken precious metals there to be sold for a goodly sum this morn, and he had told her he would more like than not be gone the whole of the day.

She smiled as Ivar wrapped his powerful arms around her, holding her close from behind. He ran a battle-calloused hand over her burgeoning belly, then let it rest there.

"I was thinking how grateful I am for our life together, of how much I love Jorvik—and of how much I love you and Eirik."

She turned in his embrace, her peaceful expression slowly dissolving into one of worry. "But Lothar will be here the soonest for the birth of our new babe and I—"

Ivar held a forefinger to her lips. "Did I not vow to act the gentleman, regardless to how your brother behaves?"

Elen closed her eyes briefly, sighing. "I just wish he would let go of Papa," she whispered. "Until he fully accepts the depth of our sire's sins, I fear he will continue to behave the boar whenever he comes to visit."

"During his last visit, he insulted me but once a day instead of once per hour."

Elen sighed.

Ivar's eyes lit up on a chuckle. "He loves you, Elen. And for that I understand his actions."

"Thank you," she said softly. "I love Lothar with all of my heart." She smiled. "But I love you even more."

His dark gaze searched her face. "You are mine and I love you," Ivar murmured. He pulled her back into his strong embrace, enveloping her in his familiar scent. Placing a sweet kiss atop her head, he assured her, "I will always love you."

Ivar had told her long ago that she was his, that she would forever belong to him. Those words, once portent, now comforted. Her husband had long since become a sure presence in an uncertain world. Whatever the fates had in store for Saxon and Viking alike, they would face the future together.

"I'm glad." Elen grinned against his chest. "Because did you try to leave me, 'twould be the last action you ever made in this realm."

"I believe you." Ivar laughed and gave her a gentle squeeze. "By the gods, I believe you!"

NEMESIS

Chapter 1

Cologne, Germany
Present day

Standing at the edge of the Rhine, Diane Sullivan took a deep breath and stared up at the docked luxury cruise ship before her. She'd never felt more nervous, vulnerable, or downright frightened in all her thirty-one years.

I can't believe I'm about to do this . . .

After absently watching seagulls fly overhead, she tucked a stray light brown curl behind one ear and stared at the ship, a surreal expression on her face. The name plastered on the side of the cruise ship in both German and English said it all: *Die Sinnliche Reise. The Carnal Voyage.*

Her stomach knotted. *What have I done?*

She was about to become a paid whore.

Okay, so she didn't *have to* have sex with the wealthy, pampered men who would be the ship's passengers when it left the dock tomorrow morning. Sex, if it happened, was her choice. But to Diane's way of thinking, her function aboard ship was too close to prostitution for her peace of mind.

Dancing, waitressing, giving massages—all with a big, submissive, welcoming smile—while she was one hundred percent, no holds barred, birthday suit *naked*. She wouldn't be able to have so much as a g-string to cover herself up with for seven days. Nothing. Nada.

Good lord.

When Diane had turned eighteen, she'd left behind the small, rural town she had called home and whisked herself off to Los Angeles with one hundred dollars and change in her pocket. She was going to be a star. Or at least that had been the plan.

Back then, naïve as it sounded today, she had believed she could have it all. She'd spent her days waiting tables and her nights dreaming of the success and fame that Hollywood would bring. Limousines, piles of money, beautiful gowns to wear to her movie debuts—maybe even a star on the Hollywood Walk of Fame one day.

Life hadn't worked out like that.

Diane knew she was a talented actress. She harbored self-doubts about many things, the normal sorts of worries and insecurities women tend to possess, but her acting ability was not among them. She was a hell of a great character actress. She knew it, her acting coach knew it, her agent knew it.

Unfortunately, she sighed, nobody else knew it.

Waiting tables all these years had barely covered the rent, let alone paid the bills. She'd worked at the trendiest eateries, but, in spite of urban legend, the Hollywood elite weren't big tippers. In fact, her healthiest tips tended to come from tourists.

Working as an extra on movie sets helped some, but not enough. The casting calls were few and far between and usually cost her more money in makeup and transportation fees than she earned. She always showed up—it was something to add to the resume if nothing else—but a cash cow it was not.

For thirteen years Diane had waited tables, worked as an extra on television and movie sets, perfected her acting ability with a coach, showed up for every audition imaginable, and waited for her big break.

And waited. And waited. And waited.

The break never came. And now, at the age of thirty-one, Diane was realistic enough to recognize that her ambitions would never be realized. It was something she should have come to terms with years ago, but she just couldn't stomach letting go.

When she was a kid, it had been the limos, dresses, and money that beckoned. And, if she was honest with herself, the belief that fame equaled love. As an adult, it was more to prove to herself and the world that her choice to leave small-town USA behind had been the right one. She'd never had a dad; after Mom died, it wasn't like there was anything left for her back home anyway.

Garek Ennis, the bane of her high school existence, had managed to shed his rural roots and make a name for himself in sports. If *that* jerk could make it, Diane had once believed, then so could she.

She couldn't have been more wrong.

Garek Ennis. An asshole and ladies' man in high school and, if the tabloids were to be believed, still an asshole and ladies' man today.

His success as a quarterback with the New York Pirates wasn't as shocking as Diane would have wished. After all, he'd been a football hero back home almost since he'd been a sperm. He was the handsomest, most muscular, most *everything* back in high school—a true golden boy with jet-black hair, sun-bronzed skin, and the greenest eyes she'd ever seen. She'd harbored a huge crush toward him. Too bad he'd also been such a jerk.

Teasing, taunting, pinching her (in those days) nonexistent breasts, Garek had been nice to the "in" girls, but he'd gone out of his way to be a royal pain in the butt to Diane. Her not being able to afford the right clothes and living on the wrong side of the tracks had made Ennis the Menace's role as The Great Humiliator all the easier.

Thankfully, Garek had been a senior when Diane started her high school freshman year. She'd only had to endure the big bully for nine and a half months before he'd left little ole Salem, Ohio, behind for college. It was hard to believe she'd ever had a crush on someone who treated her so cruelly, but there it was. She had secretly wanted Garek to like her. Instead, all he had done was use her as the butt-end of his pranks.

There was no point in thinking back on Garek. High school was water under the bridge. Still, it burned each and every time she received a disappointing phone call saying she'd lost a role to this actress or that, only to turn on the TV and see Garek's unsmiling, cocky face on the screen, a gorgeous bombshell on either arm. It was a reminder that he was and always would be what Diane Sullivan could never become: one of the beautiful people.

Hollywood looked for the latest and greatest—and youngest—fresh faces. Directors weren't interested in mature women. Never had been, never would be. Her prime had passed. With a heavy heart, she knew it was time to move on. The time had actually been years ago. But like this?

It's the only way you and Jenna can afford to start over and you damn well know it. Keep your chin up, girl. One week of embarrassment and you can start fresh in Salem where probably nobody but Carrie remembers you.

Maybe she'd become a receptionist. Or go back to school to be a dental assistant. Who knew? All Diane did know was she was putting her childhood dreams of Hollywood behind her and moving on. She had found love in Jenna, her baby girl—her raison d'etre. She didn't need fame to complete her as a person anymore.

Diane wanted things to be better for Jenna. Since Jenna's dad hadn't been interested in being a parent, Diane was the only thing her daughter had in this world. Because of that, she needed to get a real job with benefits and security. Her baby was already six years old. If the past six years were indicative of just how fast life whizzes by, before she knew what hit her, Jenna would be ready for college.

And her daughter *would* go to college. She'd have all the advantages Diane never did. All Diane had to do was get through one single, if highly humiliating, cruise, and life could begin anew.

She'd make certain Jenna never found out how low Mommy had sunk to get them out of L.A. and back to Ohio. Only Diane's best friend, Carrie, knew the truth behind this week of sin. Carrie, who was watching Jenna until Diane returned to the states, would never break a confidence like this.

One week. Seven short days . . .

The German owners of *The Carnal Voyage* had paid for her round-trip ticket. They had also paid her ten thousand dollars in cash for her nude duties—that was on top of whatever money she garnered in tips during the cruise. Diane just hoped that drunk, horny men were better tippers than the Hollywood A-list. Otherwise, this week in hell was all for nothing.

Cologne to Antwerp—and then it's all over . . .

Resigned, she blew out a breath and made her way toward the ship. Only seven days separated Diane and Jenna Sullivan from the commencement of a new life.

Seven short days.

* * *

"Jesus H. Christ! You call this piss, beer?"

Garek Ennis frowned and looked away, wondering if the German waiter even spoke English—maybe, maybe not. He sighed. Either way, there was no point in taking out his foul mood on some poor guy whose worst sin was showing up to work on a night when Garek happened to be in town.

And only a week after he'd found out that his football-playing days were over.

Garek could still hardly believe it was true. Football was all he knew. He'd lived and breathed it since he'd been a damn kid. None of that mattered in the NFL. The only thing of consequence was his shattered knee—and the fact that he could never chance being tackled again. The doctors said he'd injured it just one too many times.

Shit.

"Quit feeling sorry for yourself. We're gonna have us a good time this week. Save the bullshit 'if onlys' for later, bro."

Garek looked up into his best friend's ebony face and scowled. "That's easy for you to say, man. Nothing's keeping you from going back to the field."

Rodney and Garek had played ball together since college. Garek threw the ball; Rodney caught it and scored touchdowns. Simple as that. They'd been a hell of a team since freshman year at Ohio State. So good together, in fact, that they'd been drafted by the same team—the Pirates.

Seventeen years and two Super Bowl wins later, Garek still wasn't ready to call it quits.

"I'm getting older. My time is almost up, too," Rodney remarked. "Let it go for this week. Okay?"

Garek held his stare for a suspended moment, and then looked away. He ran a punishing hand through his closely cropped, black hair. "I'm sorry, buddy," he muttered. "I know I've been a real ass this past week and—"

"Forget it." Rodney waved it away. "That's what this week is about—forgetting things for a little while." A grin tugged at his lips. "Naked women and hot sex for seven days."

Garek glanced back at his best friend when he heard him stand up. "You heading upstairs?"

"Yeah." He wiggled his eyebrows. "I want to be good and rested up for the ladies tomorrow. See ya, bro."

Garek snorted as he watched him throw down a wad of euros and walk away. He wondered if Rodney would ever get tired of having a different woman in his bed every night of the week. Somehow he doubted it. He and Rodney were just alike in many ways, but that was one area where the similarities ended.

In the beginning, when fame and fortune had first come his way, Garek had enjoyed watching gorgeous women throw themselves at his feet. Young and horny, he'd been more than willing to oblige their desires to fuck him. He knew they'd probably wanted to screw him just so they could say they had. Like a trophy; something to tell their girlfriends maybe. Back then such a scenario had been more than fine.

That was then. This was now.

The horniness hadn't decreased with age—if anything it had only gotten worse. But for years now, fucking a different woman every night had left him feeling empty. When Doc Masters had delivered the bad news about his football career last week, that empty feeling had only escalated.

Garek's jaw tightened as his gaze drifted up from his beer to the window next to him. He absently watched the dock and the boat he'd board tomorrow, as he reflected on his life.

He was thirty-four years old. No wife. No kids. No real sense of home. He had a shitload of money, two Super Bowl rings, a yacht, three houses, and three cars. In the end, what did that mean?

Downing what was left of his lukewarm beer, Garek's gaze zeroed in on a woman walking down the dock and toward the ship. Curvaceous and busty, her hair was a long, curly, light brown threaded with golden highlights.

He squinted a bit, something about her profile sparking a weird déjà vu kind of feeling. He shifted in his seat to get a better look.

Had he fucked her before maybe? Sweet lord, there had been so many that . . .

"Diane Sullivan."

Jesus—there was a name he hadn't said aloud in years! Yeah, the woman reminded him of an older, impossibly sexier version of the prissy, clean-cut, holier-than-thou Diane Sullivan he'd known back in high school. The only girl in school who hadn't given him the time of day.

The only girl in school he'd wanted badly enough to forsake Ohio State and stay in dead-end Salem for.

At seventeen, a boy could fall fast and hard. Fourteen-turning-fifteen-year-old Diane had possessed a power over him that Garek, looking back, doubted she'd realized she had. Maybe if he'd teased her less and complimented her more?

Ahhh. That's another thing boys did at seventeen. They showed a girl they cared by behaving as stupidly as possible in her presence. It's a wonder any male ever managed to get a high school sweetheart, let alone marry one.

"You've had one too many beers tonight," Garek muttered to himself. Diane Sullivan would never work on a cruise like *that* one. Not prissy Ms. Thang.

Too bad, Garek thought bemusedly, settling back in his chair and signaling the waiter to bring him another beer. If Diane Sullivan was working on this cruise, he wouldn't have to pretend to his best friend his interest in getting on that boat and leaving Cologne tomorrow.

He'd be running to it.

Chapter 2

"All aboard!"

Naked and trembling, Diane blew out a steadying breath as she heard the captain's words echo over the intercom from her assigned station on the ship. "I can't believe this is happening," she mumbled to herself. "I will never make it through this week!"

She had thought she could do this. She had taken comfort in the knowledge that the other women on board were probably just as tense about the trip as she was and would therefore make for a great support system. Wrong on both accounts.

It had taken less than five minutes at last night's orientation for Diane to ascertain that none of the women aboard ship wanted to be acquaintances, much less friends. Other naked workers were regarded as nothing more than competition for tips. Worse, all of the other females were seasoned "ladies of leisure," true sexual aficionados.

She felt like a wallflower virgin thrown into a brothel of sex kittens.

Close to hyperventilating, she tried to figure a way out of her predicament. Unfortunately, she thought with mounting horror, there was no escape. The ten thousand dollars had already been spent! She'd used it as a down payment on a small, quaint log cabin on the rural outskirts of Salem for her and Jenna to call home.

You can do this. Calm down!

Holding her breath to the count of ten, she slowly exhaled. Her heart rate immediately came down. Thrusting her shoulders back and breasts out, Diane determined that she had come too far to back out now. Standing in a face-forward, single-file line on the upper deck, her gaze flicked to the workers below.

The nude, paid women had been told to stand in specific spots while the male clientele boarded the ship. On the lower deck, there were two lines of naked females—ten on each side. As the men began boarding, they were greeted by an army-perfect line of smiling, busty, naked women on either side of them.

A third line, the one Diane stood in, consisted of ten more side-by-side workers. Wearing nothing but high-heeled shoes of assorted colors, the women on the upper deck had been told to stand with their feet a wee bit apart—

just enough so that the men could catch a glimpse of the "treats" they had to offer as they were led underneath them to their ship-board rooms to settle in and unpack.

Diane blew out another breath as she watched the male clientele board. Her eyes widened a little as she watched them walk between the two lines of women below. They touched whomever they wanted, *wherever* they wanted, for as long as they wanted. Suddenly, she was relieved she'd been told to stand on the upper deck.

The men continued to file in. Arrogant, wealthy, and pampered, all of them had that *you-were-born-to-serve-me* look about them. Ranging from fat to heavily muscled, handsome to downright ugly, and black to white, just about every imaginable type of male was part of the ship's clientele. And insofar as Diane could tell, all of them self-importantly expected they'd be getting anything they wanted from whichever woman—or women—they wanted. For a price, of course.

"I can't believe I got myself into this," Diane muttered to herself. She was *not* like this. She didn't think she was any better or worse than the other women on board, but clearly she was not cut out for this type of job.

Seven days! Just remember, this will all be ancient history in a week.

"Calm down," the woman next to her whispered through smiling, crimson lips. She didn't look at Diane, but Diane knew that the woman was speaking to her. The other nude worker looked like a ventriloquist, trying to talk without being obvious about it. "Nothing bad will happen. You'll survive this. I've survived it three times."

Diane couldn't help but want to latch onto the only other female on ship who'd so much as spoken to her, Adrienne, she was pretty sure her name was. She barely remembered seeing her at last night's orientation, but she did recall that she'd sat on the far side of the room. Diane had tried to strike up a conversation with the two women seated close by, on either side of her, but to no avail. Both had made it clear they weren't interested in talking to her.

"Thanks," Diane whispered.

"For what?"

"For talking to me. I'm feeling very alone right now."

"*Shhhh*," Adrienne warned. "We'll talk later. Right now paste your smile on."

Having forgotten that part, Diane was grateful for the reminder. Her expression, once that of a deer caught in headlights, glowed as her lips turned up at the corners.

One of the men boarding glanced up at Diane as he made his way beneath the balcony she stood on. Dressed in a blue, pinstriped designer suit, he looked every bit the wealthy male he no doubt was. His eyes found hers and she gave him a genuine smile, an affectation more of habit and courtesy than because she wanted money from him. He winked back.

Diane watched the man look his fill at her nude body. Staring first at her face, his gaze trailed down to her large, full breasts and lingered there. An unexpected knot coiled in her belly. The coil tightened and her breasts heaved just a little as his gaze wandered down farther—over her belly, down her long legs, and then back up to her neatly trimmed, light-brown triangle of short curls. She knew he could see the folds of flesh between her legs and was taken aback by how provocative the knowledge made her feel.

Her nipples, once almost soft, poked out hard in response to his stare, a reaction that surprised her. She doubted the unexpected arousal had been born of his stare in particular, but probably from the fact that standing in the nude while a man—any man—looked at her made her feel like a reckless bad girl.

The antithesis of what she truly was.

Growing up, and all throughout her adult life, the words "reckless" and "Diane Sullivan" were oxymorons. Promiscuity had never been a part of her vocabulary. Diane knew she'd missed out on a few roles that could have made her a star because she'd always walked the straight and narrow. She didn't sleep with casting directors, agents, managers, or anyone else just because they wielded the clout that could take her to the next level.

And yet here you are, doing something you vowed you'd never do . . .

The reminder made her smile fade. The knot in her belly instantly uncoiled. She gave the man inspecting her a short, faint half-smile and looked away.

This is for Jenna. Stay strong and stand tough.

The men poured in. Her pulse raced. She realized that her mind was making it seem like there were so many more males than there really were because the small ship could carry but fifty passengers total—thirty nude female workers and twenty paying ship-goers, whose every whim would be seen to.

Two men, one white and one black, next boarded the ship in side-by-side fashion. Dressed in form-fitting jeans and t-shirts, neither was decked out in designer duds like the other patrons. Both men were incredibly muscular and in tip-top shape. Diane couldn't help but wonder why two men who looked like *that* would pay for a cruise like *this*. Surely women flung themselves at them left and right, no money required.

As the two men—presumably friends from the way they interacted—drew closer, Diane's forehead wrinkled. There was something oddly familiar about the Caucasian guy with the short black hair and the tanned, muscular physique. Something about the way he carried himself, the way he prowled onto the boat . . .

His gaze flicked up and settled on Diane. He stilled, intense eyes narrowing in déjà vu, then widening in comprehension. His jaw dropped open.

Her heart, racing madly, threatened to beat right out of her chest. Her breasts heaved up and down, drawing attention to them. He looked from her face, down to her breasts, down lower to her vagina, and back up again.

No . . . No! It can't be!

"Garek Ennis," Adrienne excitedly whispered. "There *is* a God!"

Diane was too shocked, too horrified, to speak. Adrienne might have been grateful for Garek's presence on board, but Diane was not. The bane of her high school existence was here to witness her total humiliation. She would spend seven long days on the Rhine knowing that her secret was no longer a secret. Garek could, and probably would, tell the friends he'd kept in touch with back in Salem of this cruise, and then life wouldn't begin anew for her and Jenna quite like she'd planned.

The need to bolt was all-consuming, but she didn't give in to it. Her blue gaze darted away from Garek's shocked green one. Diane took a deep breath and willed herself to ignore him.

If Adrienne was right and there *was* a God, he had a decidedly ironic sense of humor.

Garek possessed about as much enthusiasm to be on this damn boat as he did for burning holes into his skin with lit cigarettes. In a word, none. But Rodney, good ole Rodney, looked as giddy and excited as a kid on Christmas Eve. Feigning interest for his buddy's sake, Garek handed over his bags to the porter and climbed the ramp to the ship.

As he walked on board, his cock stiffened a bit despite himself. It was kind of difficult not to get a little erect when there were ten gorgeous, naked women lined up on either side of you. Brunettes, blondes, redheads, Caucasians and African Americans—every type of woman a man could possibly lust after.

His cock was semi-erect, but his enthusiasm was still running on empty. This just wasn't what he wanted anymore. Once upon a time, maybe, but not now.

Glancing up at the ten additional naked women lined in a row on the balcony above, Garek's gaze honed in on the lady he'd seen from the barroom window last night— the one who was a dead ringer for Diane Sullivan. His eyes narrowed. If he was going to fuck any woman on this ship, it would be her. It was a way to live out the one fantasy he'd never fulfilled.

Garek took his time staring at her. He stilled as her blue eyes met his. He did a double take, his eyes rounding.

Holy—Son—of—God.

That woman was no dead ringer for Diane Sullivan— she *was* Diane Sullivan! He'd known as soon as their gazes met and he saw that surprised look of identification in hers. She wasn't looking at him like that because she recognized him as Garek Ennis, football star—he'd seen that look too many times to mistake it. Diane was looking at him in a way that signified she knew him as plain old Garek Ennis from high school.

Holy shit!

Her breasts began to heave, drawing his attention. They were big and plump, and looked as sexy as he'd known they would. His gaze flicked down to her flat belly, then onward to the triangle of golden brown curls between her thighs.

Garek's cock, once semi-erect, went hard as stone. He could see everything—every nuance of what her gorgeous pussy looked like. The creases and folds, the tiny little clit . . .

He'd never been so hard in his entire life.

Diane's gaze shot away from his. Her military-straight stance told Garek she was no happier to see him now than she had been back at Salem High. Cold shoulder city.

Would she make herself available to any man aboard ship *except* for Garek? Rodney even? The thought more than annoyed him, it downright infuriated him.

If Diane Sullivan was going to fuck any man on this damn boat, it would be Garek. Period, the end.

Diane Sullivan—Jesus H. Christ! Just knowing she was here made Garek feel seventeen years old again. And he had the steel-hard erection to prove it.

Chapter 3

Alone in his room aboard *The Carnal Voyage*, Garek un-
packed his bags faster than he didn't know what. All he
wanted to do was get changed and find Diane. He couldn't
recall ever feeling this keyed up about any woman since
high school—*Diane*.

He reached for the first shirt his hands landed on and
slid into it. He frowned, wondering what exactly had happened in her life to bring her to this point. Garek had tried
to keep tabs on Diane over the years, but nobody he was
tight with back in Salem knew what had become of her. All
they could tell him was she'd hightailed it out of town the
day after graduation.

One part of Garek wanted answers, but the overriding,
far more primal part of him didn't care—he just wanted to
make certain no other man on this boat fucked her. The

rest he could find out later, maybe help her get back on her feet or whatnot.

For some women, a life like this might work. But Diane? It defied everything he'd ever known to be true about her. And back in high school, he'd made it his business to know everything about her.

"Where's my damn pants?" he growled to himself, getting irritated.

Unpacking was taking far too long. There were other males to scare off and one woman in particular to catch. The clock was ticking.

If Diane was going to be in any man's bed, it was going to be Garek's.

Diane briefly entertained fantasies of overpowering the captain and forcing him by gunpoint to dock the ship and let her disembark. Deciding that she didn't feel like doing time in a foreign prison, and recalling that she'd never held a gun in her life, much less used one to coerce a person into doing her bidding, pretty well put a damper on what seemed an otherwise great plan.

She sighed. Escape, like it or not, was impossible. All she could do now was try her damnedest to avoid Ennis the Menace.

And damn it, he looked even better in person than he did on TV! The years had only made him impossibly sexier. Tall, dark, brooding, physically powerful—the sort of larger-than-life male you saw in movies or read about in books, but never seemed to meet in reality.

She frowned. It was best not to think about Garek.

Instead she admired the ship. *The Carnal Voyage* was sleek and beautiful, the very sort of upper-class boat that Diane would have loved to have had the funds to book passage on—minus the nudity. To cruise down the Rhine, dock once a day in a new little coastal village, and enjoy the ambiance of it all . . .

These men had no clue how lucky they were. All of them were concerned with seeing naked women and getting laid—they were totally missing out on the tourist experience. Of course, all of these men were no doubt well traveled. She supposed sightseeing held little allure when you could take it for granted.

Dismissing her whimsical flight-of-fancy, Diane's thoughts returned to the present, and to the dining car she was waitressing in. She was the only woman manning this area of the ship. There had been only three customers in the dining car so far, but all three had been excellent tippers.

The other twenty-nine women were busy with their various duties, some of them giving massages, some of them dancing in the show that had commenced in the main ballroom downstairs. Adrienne had briefly popped in to wave hello, but otherwise Diane had been left alone.

At first, the staring and intimate fondling had been difficult to deal with, but an hour later she was growing more accustomed to it and able to blank out her mind so she didn't care. She had known when she signed up for the cruise that the patrons would be allowed to touch her anywhere they wanted without permission. Letting that happen in theory and in reality were two entirely different matters, but she was getting better at blocking everything out.

Placing the sandwiches, pasta salads, and drinks two men had ordered on a tray, Diane picked it up and walked over to the table where they were seated. She plastered on a smile as she began unloading the food and drinks, placing the proper meals in front of customers four and five.

"Is there anything else I can get for you gentlemen right now or will this do it?"

They both grinned in a way to suggest there was a lot more she could serve them—if willing. Diane had to force herself not to blush.

"Well," one of them spoke up, his Italian accent thick, "hopefully later, bella." He placed a single finger just over her navel and made a soft trail down to her triangle of curls. "Very beautiful," he murmured.

"Hello!" a new male voice growled, demanding Diane's attention. He used a fork to chime on a wine glass at his table in a distinctly irritating fashion. "I'd like to order some food, too."

Diane glanced up—and paled. Her pulse soared just as it had out on the balcony earlier in the day.

Garek.

What was he doing here? Diane wondered, horrified. She thought he would be more interested in the shows and massages than in sandwiches and appetizers in a practically empty dining car. Diane had been warned that her station wouldn't pick up until after the shows had ended and the men got hungry. Even then, most of them would order room service, preferring to have naked females come to their bedrooms solo in the hopes of luring them into giving out more than trays of food.

Diane's boss, seeing her reticence, had assigned her to the least popular area of the ship. She was fine by that— had welcomed it even—for she realized she just wasn't up to snuff where most of the ship's activities were concerned. She had hoped it would be otherwise, but accepted that this was as wild as she could get.

She had assumed this dining car would keep her far away from Garek. Apparently, she had assumed wrong.

"I'll check back with you two gentlemen in a few minutes," Diane managed to get out. She willed her heart to stop beating so dramatically. "Enjoy your lunch."

The walk to Garek's table felt like a death march, paradoxically the longest and shortest walk of Diane's life. He was dressed in casual elegance, sleek black trousers and a blue silk shirt that showed off his massive, vein-roped biceps. Unlike in high school when he'd worn his jet-black hair a bit on the long side, his current style was short and neatly cropped. Those eyes hadn't changed a bit, though. They were as jungle-green and intimidating as ever.

And lordy how those eyes were looking at her now. They missed nothing, saw everything. Garek inspected her from the top of her long, light-brown, curly hair, which she'd wound into a loose bun with curls softly cascading down her shoulders, to the bottom of her red, high-heeled shoes. His gaze stopped at her breasts, watched them jiggle as she walked, before traveling lower, taking in the sight of her light-brown triangle of neatly trimmed curls.

Against her will, her body reacted to his stare. Her nipples beaded into tight points and that knot coiled in her belly once again. This time the knot didn't form from being watched by any man, but from one man in particular.

She took a deep breath and slowly exhaled. Standing before Garek totally naked, Diane gave him a faint smile. Maybe out on the balcony she had imagined that he recognized her from high school. Perhaps he had no clue who she was! Diane held on tight to that hope and plowed on. "Welcome to the Jungle Room. What would you like to order?"

A blowjob? Three hours with my face buried between your thighs? The hardest, roughest, longest fuck of my life? Let me get you pregnant?

"A beer," Garek said a bit gruffly. He cleared his throat. "For now."

"House draft?"

"That's fine."

She nodded and walked off. Garek blew out a breath, the sight of her naked, perfectly rounded ass as much a turn-on as her tits and pussy were. When she accidentally dropped a napkin and had to bend over to retrieve it, he thought he'd come right in his pants.

She was even sexier than he'd fantasized her to be. So many hours in his youth he'd spent in the shower pumping his cock with his hand while dreaming of seeing Diane Sullivan naked. Now she was here. And very, very naked.

By the time she started walking toward him with his beer in her hand, perspiration had broken out on his forehead. Her breasts were definitely D-cup, her nipples large and rosy-pink.

She leaned over the table. Garek's heavy-lidded gaze flicked from the nipples a few scant inches away from his mouth up to her face as she set the glass in front of him. "How are you, Diane?" he murmured.

Her face paled. Did she think he didn't recognize her? He frowned, recalling that she probably hoped he hadn't. No, the Diane he had known would definitely not want to be spotted on a cruise like this.

It took her a moment to gather herself together, but eventually her shoulders straightened. To her credit, she was blushing profusely, but still managed to be polite.

"I'm just fine, Garek. How are you?"

Horny. "Never been better," he lied.

She gave him a half-hearted smile while avoiding his gaze. "I'm glad. Would you like to order some food, too, or just the beer?"

His jaw tightened. She was making it perfectly clear

that she was no more interested in him now than she had been back in high school.

Or was she? Maybe she was just embarrassed that someone who knew her had seen her on this boat naked as the day she was born.

Either way, Diane didn't want to get involved in conversation. For now, he'd let it go.

"Beer's fine. I'll get some food after I finish it."

Her woefully inept attempt at cheerfulness all but made his teeth grind. "Great. I'll check back on you in a few minutes."

And then she was gone, walking back over to where the Italians were seated. He felt like a little kid, sulking because her attention was on everyone and anyone but him—where it belonged.

An hour became two, two became three, and still Garek didn't leave. Diane was getting increasingly nervous. And, as loathe as she was to admit it, increasingly aroused. His green eyes followed her everywhere, watching her with an intensity that bordered on possessiveness.

At first, she'd been ready to faint dead away every time she felt his searing gaze on her. After a while, she'd actually found herself relishing his stare. This was, after all, the same man who had gone out of his way to make her life hell back in Salem—now it was obvious he wanted her.

Probably only for a night, but he clearly wanted her. He wasn't going to get a kiss from her, let alone make his way into her bed, but Diane was enjoying the feeling of being wanted by her high school crush in this moment.

Unless he decided to up the ante and touch her.

Garek had that right on this ship and he'd yet to exercise it. She wasn't certain how she'd react if he touched her. Hopefully he wouldn't and the what-ifs would be a moot point.

"Hey," a busty, blonde, female said to Diane as she entered the dining car. "I'm here to relieve you. Boss says you get an hour break."

Diane glanced up at her. "Thanks." She smiled. "I'm Diane."

"Good for you," the woman said flippantly. The obvious brush-off hurt Diane more than she wanted it to. "Just be back in an hour. I hate working in the dining car. Shitty tips."

Diane sighed and left the Jungle Room. She gave Garek a weak smile as she passed by his table and kept walking.

It took her a minute to orient herself. Her bedroom was downstairs and off the starboard wing. En route, she passed the ballroom and caught a glimpse of the sex show going on. Her eyes widened as she watched naked, oiled-down women jiggle their breasts in the patrons' faces, writhe up and down on their laps, thrust their nipples into awaiting mouths . . .

Sweet lord, she was glad she'd been assigned to the dining car. Diane shook her head, straightened her shoulders,
and resumed walking. She rounded a bend and made her
way down the corridor leading to her bedroom.

A curious feeling stole over Diane, an intuition that told
her she was being watched. She ignored the feeling, realizing that any number of men could be staring at her, and
strode up to her bedroom door.

Just as she was preparing to sink the key into the lock,
two strong hands slapped against the wood at either side of
her face and didn't budge. A huge erection poked against
her back.

Diane gasped, then turned around. Her eyes widened
when she realized whose embrace she was trapped in. Her
heartbeat worked triple time. "Garek," she breathed out.

His intense stare penetrated every atom of her being.
His eyelids were heavy as his gaze wandered up and down
the length of her. "I've been wanting you my whole damn
life," he said thickly.

Diane had no time to react to that astonishing an-
nouncement. One moment he was staring at her and the
next his mouth roughly came down on top of hers. He
kissed her breathlessly, mercilessly, as his large, calloused
hands roamed the length of her nude body. He took his
time and felt her everywhere, his palms massaging her
breasts, her belly, then grabbing her buttocks and kneading
them like dough.

She moaned into his mouth, her entire body on fire. He tore his lips away from hers and, breathing heavily, let go of her ass and grabbed both breasts. Garek stared at her nipples for a lingering moment, and then drew one into the heat of his mouth.

Diane gasped as he sucked on her nipple, the knot in her belly coiling so tight she almost came. He must have been a breast man, for he spent an ungodly amount of time sucking on them, popping one and then the other into his mouth, drawing on them, tugging them with his teeth, making her writhe and moan against him.

"Garek."

He released a nipple with a popping sound, then kissed his way down her belly. He went down on his knees in front of her and slid his tongue along the slit of her vagina. She groaned as she opened her legs a bit more, the thought that she was standing in the hallway for anyone to see not even registering.

Garek used his fingers to spread her lips apart. "My God," he growled, staring at her flesh, "you've got a gorgeous, tight cunt, Diane."

Her heart felt like a rock pounding against her breasts. She instinctively threaded her fingers through his dark hair as he took her clit into his mouth and sucked it hard.

"Oh, God," Diane moaned, pressing his face against her pussy. *"Garek."* He sucked on her clit harder, the pressure overwhelming.

Diane Sullivan was about to come for Garek Ennis whether she wanted to or not.

She burst on a loud moan, her nipples stabbing out as she rode the sensual wave to its crescendo. Blood rushed to her face, heating it, and to her nipples, elongating them.

By the time Garek finished lapping up her juices, she could barely stand. Her heart was drumming madly, her legs as steady as rubbery noodles.

Garek took the key out of her hand, and Diane swallowed roughly as she watched him open her bedroom door for her. Would he come inside? Would he make love to her?

"I'll see you later," Garek murmured, his eyes blazing. She could smell the scent of her arousal all over his jaw and mouth. "Don't ever ignore me again, sweetheart."

Chapter 4

Don't ever ignore me again, sweetheart.

It was a day later and Diane was still sitting in her bedroom brooding. Uncertain as to how she should feel, and depressed because of it, she'd feigned illness and called in sick last night.

Her heart had soared when Garek said he'd been wanting her his entire life. Had that been a lie? Had he done what he'd done to her yesterday because he truly wanted her, or because Garek Ennis, superstar quarterback, couldn't stand to be ignored?

She'd never felt so vulnerable in her entire life. Garek might have been the bane of her freshman year in high school, but he'd also been her first, and if she was honest with herself, deepest, crush.

"Achoo!"

Diane's sneeze made the light bulb in her mind flick on. If she could pretend to be ill last night, she could do the same this afternoon.

And what will tomorrow's excuse be, smart one? How many days can you possibly pretend to be ill? Mr. Heinzman could ask for his ten thousand dollars back!

She promised herself that no matter how scared she felt tomorrow, she would not call in. Just this once. Only one more time.

Diane needed just a wee bit more mental preparation before she was forced to see Garek again. She still wasn't ready. Feigning a case of the sniffles, she picked up the phone and called her boss.

Where are you, Diane?

The urge to see her was overpowering. He wanted to kiss her again, to touch her again. Hell, even just talking to her would suffice at the moment! Not that he didn't want to talk to her. He had a million questions stored up to ask her, sixteen years' worth of them.

Realizing he wasn't the best talker in the world—his typical response was a one- or two-word grunt—Garek figured he stood a better chance at snagging Diane without words than with them. It was kind of hard to try either scenario, though, when the woman he was hunting had managed to elude him—again.

She hadn't shown up for work last night and he'd yet to

see her today. Diane had avoided him with painful accuracy sixteen years ago and she was doing it again now.

What if she's not avoiding you? What if another man on this ship seduced her into his bed?

His jaw tightened. *Can we say "death row"?* He'd strangle any man who touched her.

Impatient, and feeling as territorial as a lion prepared to fight for his superiority in the alpha chain, Garek stomped off to find Mr. Heinzman.

He wanted answers, and he wanted them now.

Diane's eyes went wide as she listened to Mr. Heinzman's terrifying words over the telephone connection. "But I'm sick. And I thought I was working the dining car anyway," she said a bit shakily.

"You were. You didn't show up—twice—so I had to re-assign it. Now we're short a masseuse."

"But I don't know how to give massages!"

"Learn. Quickly. You've only got one customer tonight, then maybe I can put you back in the dining car tomorrow."

"Mr. Heinzman, I really don't think—"

"I sent the porter up with the key to room seventeen. He should be there any minute."

And she had thought facing Garek was bad? Holy God! How would she get through this? Whatever man she was going to massage probably would expect sex afterward. This was terrible!

Diane felt like she was going to faint. Or vomit. "I understand," she said a bit weakly.

"Good. Because you haven't been earning your keep. Massage him for an hour."

Mr. Heinzman slammed down the phone. Diane's heart sank. She really had no choice but to give the massage. As much as she despised the old pervert at the moment, he was correct: a deal was a deal and she wasn't keeping her part very well.

A knock at the door startled Diane. *The porter.* Closing her eyes, she took a deep breath and quickly prepared herself to get through the next hour.

It was either that or come up with ten thousand dollars that she didn't have.

Chapter 5

Diane was trembling by the time she reached room seventeen. She'd never given a massage in her life, much less to a man while she was totally naked. This entire cruise was already getting to be too much—and it was only day two! She still had five horrid days to make it through.

Taking a calming breath, Diane stood before room seventeen with its key in hand. Deciding that she may as well get it over with, she sank the key into the lock and opened the door.

An hour. Only sixty measly minutes . . .

Entering the bedroom, she was taken aback by how lavish it was. Much different from the small, cramped quarters she'd been given to use. The living room was palatial, with a beautiful balcony that overlooked the Rhine leading off of it.

Her eyes flicked to the empty massage table set in the middle of the living room. Apparently whoever occupied this room was in the bathroom or bedroom, yet another difference from Diane's quarters—her bedroom, bathroom, and living room were all in one very confined space. The suites for the paying passengers were beyond gorgeous.

"Hello?" She cleared her throat, her voice sounding shaky even to her. "Is anybody here?"

A freshly showered man emerged from the master bedroom wearing nothing but a scant white towel around his middle. Diane stilled as she instantly recognized who the man was. Her eyes widened.

"Garek."

She forced herself to swallow, her mouth dry as cotton. The man looked powerful and dangerous when fully clothed, but while wearing nothing but a towel, his every deadly muscle there to see? Her heartbeat picked up in the dramatic tempo it reserved for Garek's presence alone. Tall, tan, and heavy with muscle, his body was undeniably in its prime.

Garek.

Diane could hardly believe it. Was this just a coincidence? Or had he asked Mr. Heinzman for her specifically?

His gaze glanced over Diane's mons and breasts before settling on her face. Her nipples stabbed out at his inspection. "Expect to be here a while," he said softly, his voice almost a purr. Did she faint now or later? "I feel pretty tense."

Diane's smile was faint. "I guess we've finally found something in common then."

Garek took his time looking up and down the length of Diane. Sweet lord, she was beautiful. Even prettier now than she'd been in high school. His cock was so hard he knew she could see the tent in his towel. His suspicion was confirmed when she blushed and looked away.

The desire to carry her into the bedroom and fuck her like a madman was powerful, but he'd decided at the moment his eyes had first met hers on the balcony that he was going to take this as slowly as possible. *As possible* being the key words here. There was only so much teasing a man could take. Standing this close to the object of his sixteen-years-long obsession and desire was testing his limits of endurance and she hadn't even laid a crimson-manicured fingertip on him yet.

This had the makings of a very long night.

She cleared her throat. "Shall uh . . . shall we get started then?"

Garek didn't answer Diane with words, but with actions. Moving his hands from his hips in the football player stance he favored, to the tip of the towel just under his navel, he took the scant piece of garment off and flung it away from him.

As if she couldn't help herself, Diane took a peek at his

cock. Her eyes widened a bit, a reaction that made him impossibly harder—and hornier.

"About ten inches," Garek murmured. "In case you were wondering."

Her blush deepened, forcing him to suppress a grin. Diane Sullivan was not only gorgeous, but she was cute, too.

"It—err—it never crossed my mind."

She was lying. He didn't know how he knew; he just did.

"Too bad." He walked over to the massage table and hopped up on it. He sighed. "Might as well get started then."

Her voice was weak, but audible. "Right. Okay then."

She cleared her throat before nervously walking toward him. Garek stretched out on the massage table as best he could, back toward the floor, cock toward the ceiling.

"Ummm . . ." Diane cleared her throat again.

He lifted one dark eyebrow, feigning ignorance. He already knew what she was going to ask.

"Aren't you—aren't I—"

"Yes?"

"Aren't you supposed to lie on your stomach?" she finally squeaked out.

Garek shrugged. "I don't want my back massaged. I want my front massaged." *Especially my hard-on, but I'll settle for anything at the moment!* "Are you going to get started?"

She looked like a deer caught in headlights. Had he said she was cute? "Adorable" was a better word.

"Yes." She blinked, then looked around for the massage oil. Espying it under the table, she let out a none too subtle breath as she marched toward him. Her tits jiggled with the movements, making pre-cum spill from the tip of his erection.

I'm going to explode as soon as she touches me. Control yourself, control yourself, control yourself . . .

His jaw tightened at first contact. Feeling her oiled-down hands touch his chest was sheer heaven. He breathed in deeply and exhaled as he felt her fingers massage his neck and chest. His gaze darted to the hard nipples dangling just inches above his mouth. Unable to resist, he lifted his head long enough to draw one into his mouth and give it a quick suck. She gasped when he released it, but didn't look at him.

"You're sexy as hell, Diane," Garek growled.

"Thank you," she said quickly. She blinked several times in rapid succession. "So are you."

His heart soared at her words. It was the first verbal encouragement she'd given him—ever.

Her hands moved lower, to his six-pack belly. Garek sucked in his breath when a few of her fingers accidentally— or purposefully—brushed against the head of his erection. "You're killing me, Diane," he rasped.

A fire ignited her blue eyes, a look that could only be described as devilish. Her hands found his cock and squeezed, surprising him. He groaned as she began to masturbate him; he was already this close to coming.

"Do you like this?" she murmured, going from demure

girl to unabashed woman in what seemed like the blink of an eye. "Does it feel good?"

His jaw was so tense it felt close to cracking. "Yes," Garek gritted out. His cock throbbed in her hands, threatening to erupt at any moment.

"You're very big," she whispered, making him breathe deeply. "I don't know if I can handle something so big."

Sweet lord, her words came straight out of his high school fantasies. There was but a single remaining detail missing.

"I guess there's only one way to find out."

The remaining detail had been found.

Breathing heavily, every muscle in his body tensed up as her face neared his cock. "Oh God, Diane," Garek gasped. *"Shit."*

Her crimson-stained lips enveloped the head of his erection. He bucked up, having never felt so hard and out of control in his life. She took him in deeper, all the way, until he swore he was touching tonsils. He closed his eyes on a moan.

"Suck harder." His eyes flicked open as he reached out for Diane's head and sifted his fingers through her long, light-brown hair. "Christ," he ground out, "this feels so damn good, baby."

The more worked up and encouraging Garek became, the bolder Diane got. She sucked him off mercilessly, head to root, faster and harder. The sucking sounds of mouth meeting cock reached his ears. She began to moan a little in the back of her throat, a soft *Mmmmm* sound that all but drove him over the edge.

"I'm going to come, baby," Garek said thickly.

He could barely keep his eyes open, but forced himself to so he didn't miss a beat. Watching his erection disappear into the depths of Diane Sullivan's throat was the most erotic sight he'd ever seen. His cock began to jerk and throb, letting him know it was time.

Her head bobbed up and down, her lips and tongue ruthlessly working him. His hand held the back of her head, pushing her face into him as close as humanly possible. He wanted the ecstasy to last forever, but he was beyond the point of turning back.

"Shit!" Garek roared, every muscle in his body tensing. *"Diane."*

He came hard, violently, his body convulsing on a groan. Hot cum spurted out of his cock like a geyser, a huge eruption that put all previous orgasms combined to shame.

"Diane," he rasped, his breathing heavy. His toes curled as he watched her lick up his juices, swallowing every drop. "Diane, you are so sexy."

He had just come and he was already getting hard again. He wanted to fuck her more than he wanted to breathe.

But more importantly, he wanted her to realize this was going to be much more than a *fuck-til-the-cruise-ends* kind of thing. Garek had never thought to see Diane again. Now that she was back in his life, there was no way she was ever leaving it again.

NEMESIS

"Thank you," he said with paradoxically gentle roughness. His gaze found hers. "I've been fantasizing about that since high school."

She didn't know what had possessed her to behave as she had, but the timidity was returning now that Garek had come. Luckily, not so bad as before. A woman could only be so shy after sucking off a man she'd known most of her life.

Diane Sullivan had just given Garek Ennis a blowjob. What's more, he had said he'd been fantasizing about her doing that very thing to him for years and years. Good grief.

A part of her was elated by the confession. Another part was saddened because she had never thought to see Garek again after he left for college, but now she was seeing him as a paid whore. This wasn't a part of her dreams, those secret longings she'd harbored all of these years about making it big in Hollywood and *then* encountering Ennis the Menace.

Still, Garek was being very gracious about the entire situation. She wasn't mad at him because he wasn't treating her like a paid whore. She was just disappointed in herself, and fate in general.

"You're welcome," Diane said quietly. She sighed resignedly and straightened up. Unsure what to do or say, she began putting away the massage oil. "I didn't do that for money," she told him, her voice subdued, "so don't you dare give me any."

Silence.

"Will you go out on a date with me tomorrow?" Garek asked, surprising her. Her gaze darted back to his face. "You know, a real one. The boat is leaving Germany tonight and docking for a few hours in Holland tomorrow. I'd like to spend that time with you."

Her heart began to beat dramatically in her chest. Back in high school, a blowjob might have been Garek's fantasy, but a real date had been hers.

"That would be very nice," she heard herself say. She smiled, the first genuine smile she'd given him since the cruise began. "I'd love to."

Chapter 6

Getting dressed for his date with Diane, Garek felt like a giddy little kid. The only things missing from the picture were, thankfully, the acne and doofy eighties clothing. He wore a long-sleeved hunter-green shirt and black trousers, and his heart was beating with anticipation by the time he knocked on Diane's cabin door. The smile she gave him made him hard as a rock—no surprise there.

"Wow." Garek looked her up and down, his erection painful. Only Diane could make a simple cotton sundress and brown sandals look so damn good. "You're beautiful."

"Thanks." She took a deep breath and blew it out. "I'm so excited. I've never been to Holland before. Or anywhere for that matter."

He felt his own excitement rising at her confession. He rather liked the idea of showing her places she'd never seen before. Stupid, maybe, but there it was.

"Doesn't Heinzman ever give you time off?" he growled.

Diane blushed and he immediately knew he'd said the wrong thing. "We're allowed only one day off the entire trip. This is my first—and last—cruise," she weakly admitted, looking down at her shoes. "I guess you could say I needed the money, but didn't realize until I got here that I didn't need it that badly."

His heart soared at her words. Truth be told, he didn't care if Diane was a seasoned prostitute or a blushing virgin. He wanted to be with her no matter what. Still, the possessive streak in him liked her words, more than a lot.

His eyes searched her face. "You don't have to explain yourself, Diane," he murmured. "If you hadn't signed up to work this cruise I might never have gotten the chance to see you again."

She blushed as she met his gaze, but smiled. More importantly, she seemed like she was finally easing up in his presence, at least a little. A small, but significant, step. "Shall we go then?"

He winked, and took her hand in his. "This way, milady. Holland awaits you."

* * *

The village they docked in, Gouda, was quaintly fascinating. Famous for its cheese, candles, and Gothic townhall, Diane felt like she'd walked into a picture book. Garek pointed out different sights and took the time to show her most of them. They did everything from watching cheese being made to oohing and ahhing at the painted glass windows of St. John's church. Diane couldn't recall having ever had so much fun.

More than that, she couldn't believe she was on a real date with Garek Ennis. This day came straight out of her high school fantasies. Back then she had wanted him to take her to the movies and Salem's fanciest restaurant. This was a much better reality than her fevered teenage mind could have dreamt up.

You make me feel like a hopeful young girl again, Garek. I don't think I had butterflies in my stomach like this even in high school, though.

When there was only a single hour left until they had to return to the ship, they wound their way down the narrow streets of Gouda and back toward the dock. There they had lunch in a little pub overlooking the river.

"So," Garek said, inclining his head at Diane when their drinks were set in front of them, "tell me what you've been up to. I tried to find you after you graduated from high school, but nobody knew where you'd hied yourself off to."

He had tried to find her? Her heart soared. "L.A." Diane smiled and told him about her acting aspirations that had never come to pass. "But that's okay. I guess it just wasn't meant to be."

"I'm sorry," he said sincerely. "I'm sure you would have made a great actress."

She shrugged, not really wanting to talk about it. The wound was still too fresh. "I finally got smart, gave up the dream, and decided to move back to Ohio to give Jenna and me a fresh start."

"Jenna?"

Diane's heart was in her eyes. "My daughter."

"I didn't know you had a daughter. How old is she?"

"Six." Diane chuckled. "She acts like six going on sixteen half the time."

Garek's eyes searched hers. "That's really cool, Diane," he murmured. "I'd love to meet Jenna someday. Assuming her dad wouldn't mind?"

Diane quickly expelled him of that worry. She wasn't certain why she cared enough to do so and didn't particularly feel up to analyzing it. "He doesn't want anything to do with Jenna. He's never even seen her."

Garek sighed, frowning. "I'm sorry, Diane. It sounds like you've had a tough go of it."

"No need to be sorry," she assured him. "Jenna and I do great solo."

Garek was silent for a protracted moment and then said, "Can I ask you a question?"

She sighed, already knowing what it was. "You don't want to be rude, but you want to know how I ended up working this cruise. Right?"

He ran a hand over his jaw and glanced away. "Something like that," he muttered. He looked back, meeting her gaze. "I was, uh—shocked. To put a fine point on it."

"Me, too." She rolled her eyes self-deprecatingly and grinned. "I thought this cruise would be an easy way to earn the down payment on the log cabin I bought in Ohio. You know, a nest-egg for me and Jenna to have while we start anew." She shook her head, her smile fading, and blew out a breath. "The cruise was a lot easier in thought than in deed. I had no idea that seven days would feel like seven years."

His chuckle was soft and made laugh lines appear at the corners of his eyes, an effect Diane found charming. Not to mention sinfully handsome. "I'll just bet." He grew serious then, his hand finding hers atop the table and gently covering it. "But I'm glad you signed up for it."

Their gazes met and locked. Diane's pulse picked up in tempo. "Me too," she whispered.

He looked as though he was preparing to kiss her. Nibbling on her lower lip, she held his stare for an intense moment, then glanced away. "I'd ask what you've been up to for the past sixteen years, but I doubt there is a soul alive who doesn't already know. At least in the United States. Sounds like you're leading a very exciting life."

He frowned. Because she'd avoided his kiss? Because she'd made his life sound more idyllic than it was? She didn't know.

"Exciting? No. That part faded away a long time ago."

Her eyebrows drew together. His words had sounded tired, weary. "I—I'm sorry," she said a bit awkwardly, unsure of what to say. "The papers make your life sound like one big party."

"In the beginning it was—I'd be lying if I said otherwise. But that was years ago, Diane," he murmured. "Many, many years ago. Now what I've got is a lot of money, very few real friends, and a shattered knee."

"Shattered knee?"

He sighed, and smiled sadly. "The doctor says I can't risk playing ball ever again."

Silence.

"I'm sorry, Garek," Diane whispered.

She felt like a true jerk for all the mean thoughts she'd harbored of him before they'd become reacquainted. All this time she'd envied him for making a name for himself when she hadn't, only to find out he didn't really have anything in his life worth holding on to anymore. At least Diane had Jenna. Her daughter meant a whole hell of a lot more than money ever could.

His gaze found hers. "Thank you," he said quietly. "That means a lot."

Uncomfortable with the ensuing silence, Diane smiled,

then glanced away. Her gaze landed on an ornate wall-mounted timepiece. Her smile fell.

Five o'clock. Time to board. This is when Cinderella turns back into the soot-covered peasant girl . . .

Garek turned his head to see what Diane was staring at. "Damn," he growled. "Today flew by."

"It did." Diane blinked, then looked at him. "Thank you for a truly memorable day, Garek." Her smile was luminous. "I'll never forget this time with you if I live to be eighty."

One dark eyebrow shot up. "You say that like it's goodbye?"

"I—"

"Here is your bill, sir," a waitress cut in. Her Dutch accent was thick. "Unless there is anything else I can get for you two?"

"No," Garek snapped. He ran a hand over his jaw, regaining his patience. "But thank you."

Diane gently cleared her throat. Pulse racing, she decided she didn't want to continue the conversation they'd been engaged in before the waitress interrupted them. This day had been like magic, a dream come true. She didn't want reality to ruin it. There was plenty of time for that.

"Well," Diane breathed out, shooting up from her seat, "I guess we'd better get back to the ship before it leaves without us."

Garek stared at her for a suspended moment before standing up and throwing down a wad of euros on the table. Diane's heart sank as she followed him in silence from the bistro.

Chapter 7

Diane paced in her tiny room aboard *The Carnal Voyage*, disappointed by her earlier actions. Back in the pub Garek had asked her if this was goodbye—she felt like throttling herself for not screaming, "*Nooooo!*" and throwing herself into his awaiting, masculine arms.

She frowned. The acting aspirations were dead, perhaps, but apparently she still harbored something of a dramatic streak.

She plopped down onto the bed with a sigh, chin in her palm. She didn't want it to be goodbye. Not by a long shot. She wanted more time to spend with him, for it meant more memories to take with her.

Diane wasn't certain what had caused her to choke in Garek's presence back in the pub—it wasn't her style. The only explanation that seemed up to snuff was that he really did make her feel like the shy, quiet, hopelessly enamored Diane Sullivan she'd been back in high school.

If you possessed half a brain, you'd let him go. Preferably before you fall in love with him all over again . . .

Such an outcome was more than possible and she knew it. There was something special about a woman's first crush. She could have never run into Garek again and he still would have owned a little piece of her heart until the day she took her last breath.

"Let him go," Diane whispered to the walls of her bedroom.

When the cruise was over, Garek would go back to New York, or L.A., or wherever it was he now owned homes, and resume his glitzy life. Diane would return to Salem, Ohio, and be a mom to Jenna and a best friend to Carrie.

Diane flopped over on her back and closed her eyes. She wouldn't go back to L.A. even if she had something— or someone—to go back to. She wanted Jenna to have a safe upbringing in a small town where you didn't have to schlep several miles just to see a blade of grass.

Painful as it was, it was time to face facts: her life couldn't be more different from Garek's.

Opposites attract, but similars stay together.

"I don't see what the problem is." Rodney sat down in the chair next to Garek's. They were having a beer together in Garek's private stateroom. "If you feel that strongly about her, then go tell her." He frowned. "I've never seen you act like such a pussy before, bro."

"Gee, thanks."

"You know what I mean."

Garek grunted. Yeah, he did. It wasn't like him to get nervous about whether or not Lady A, B, or C wanted him to keep hanging around. Of course, that could have had something to do with the fact that they typically wanted him to stay. It wasn't just ego saying this, but experience.

Except where Diane was concerned. Garek's jaw clenched. Deviations from the norm always seemed to come right back to her. He had no ego at all when it came to Diane—never had—and was beginning to wonder if he ever would.

"Yes, I know what you mean." Garek tipped the bottle up to his lips and finished it. Setting it down, he decided to change subjects. He'd dwell on Diane later, when he was alone. "You enjoying yourself?"

Rodney shrugged. "I guess."

One black eyebrow shot up. Garck had thought a cruise like this would be a dream come true for his best friend.

"I don't know," Rodney sighed. "I must be getting old, because I've spent more time on the balcony of my room watching the river than I have fucking."

Garek chuckled. "Could be a sign of something other than old age. I've been afflicted by this disease myself and it's only gotten worse since I was reacquainted with Diane."

"Disease?"

"Yeah. It's called growing up."

Rodney snorted. "I hear you, bro." He stood up to fetch himself a cup of coffee. "I never thought I'd live to say this, but I'm sick of casual sex."

It occurred to Garek that in all the years they'd been best friends, they rarely had heart-to-heart talks. As a result, the entire conversation felt a little stiff. Maybe women talked to their girlfriends like this all the time, but guys just didn't.

Searching for a meaningful response, all Garek could come up with was a mumbled, "Me, too."

Rodney sat back down with his coffee. They stared at each other for a minute. "So what are you going to do?" he finally asked.

Garek didn't know. He wished he did. Unfortunately, Diane was the Queen of Mixed Signals. He wasn't certain that she wanted him in her life.

Or maybe she hadn't crossed her wires. Maybe Garek was just having trouble reading them for the first time since high school. He couldn't recall ever feeling this unsure of where he stood with a woman.

"I'm going to have a cup of coffee, too," Garek said, frowning. A situation like this couldn't be rushed. He had a lot of thinking to do. "You want cream and sugar for yours?"

Tired from pacing and overwrought nerves, Diane fell asleep on the tiny bed in her equally tiny bedroom. When she awoke a couple of hours later, it was to the knowledge that she was all alone and only had herself to thank.

Garek had made it clear back in the pub that he wanted to see Diane again. Diane's avoidance of the subject had all but told him that she didn't return his sentiment. If she were in Garek's shoes and a man had reacted to her the way she had reacted to him, Diane recognized that she would have believed he wasn't interested in seeing her again.

She stiffened. It wasn't like her to be a weeping willow and she didn't plan to assume that role now. If she let Garek walk out of her life without telling him how she felt, she'd never forgive herself.

Bolting up off the bed, Diane rummaged in her closet for something to wear. In a hurry, she chose a white t-shirt and jeans.

She wasn't supposed to amble around *The Carnal Voyage* with clothes on, but she didn't want to do the walk from her bedroom to Garek's stateroom naked. Another paying passenger might try to stop her en route and she wasn't up for the attention at the moment.

"I want off this damn boat already," Diane mumbled to the four walls, trying to work up her nerve to go to Garek. *This is just too much!*

She made her way to the bathroom so she could freshen up her I-just-tumbled-out-of-bed appearance. Diane was scared to tell him the truth about her awakening feelings, but conceded that she had to. She had never loved any man the way she had loved Garek in high school. Seeing him again was making all the magical, butterflies-in-the-belly feelings come crashing back.

He wielded the power to hurt her, something she'd never thought would happen again where Garek was concerned. Nevertheless, she owed it to herself—and to him—to find out how he felt about her.

Ennis the Menace wasn't getting off the ship without knowing how Diane Sullivan felt about him.

Rodney had long since departed, leaving Garek to his tumultuous thoughts. Should he go to Diane's room and tell her he wanted to see her again—be with her forever if he had his way—or should he stay put and see if she came to him?

The first possibility opened him up for humiliation. The second one could result in never seeing Diane again.

Garek ran a punishing hand through his short, black hair and sighed. Whether or not Diane wanted to see him again, he didn't want her to leave the ship without knowing his feelings.

He had loved her with his whole heart as a gawky kid. When he sat back and really thought about it, he couldn't sincerely say that the feelings had ever died. More like lain in waiting.

Over the years Garek had contrasted every girlfriend against the way he'd felt back in high school when he was near Diane. Inevitably, those women had always paled by comparison. Nobody could make his heart race or put adolescent butterflies in his belly.

Except for Diane.

Garek's jaw clenched as he began to pace back and forth in his stateroom. There was only one viable course to take, and he had known all along what it was. He had to go to Diane's room and tell her how he felt about her. If she left the boat without knowing, he'd curse himself until the day he died.

Chapter 8

Garek had never felt so determined in his life. Dressed in a black silk shirt and black pants, he marched over to Diane's room. He had done a lot of thinking in the last few hours and there was no way in hell he was letting her get away that easily.

They had enjoyed a great time together in Gouda. He wanted there to be a lot more of those times.

Prepared to knock on her door, Garek's hand found air instead as the door flew open. Diane yelped, obviously taken by surprise.

"Garek," she breathed out, her blue eyes wide and sexy, "what are you doing here?"

His gaze raked over her. Damn, she looked good. She wore a white t-shirt and jeans, no bra to impede the view.

Her ripe nipples poked against the cotton, giving him an instant erection.

In contrast to her tousled clothes, her makeup and hair were perfectly done. Garek ached to dishevel them.

His heart was racing. Those damn butterflies he experienced only in Diane's presence were back again.

Their gazes clashed and held. Her breasts heaved up and down in time with her unsteady breathing. She wanted him. He wanted to tell her how he felt, but the words wouldn't come. He'd never been good with words. Actions, however, were his specialty.

One minute she was standing before him and the next she was in his arms. He growled as his mouth demandingly came down on hers, kissing her with all the passion he felt inside. She moaned into his mouth, driving him wild with desire.

There was no time for foreplay. They'd indulged in it for days now. Garek needed to fuck her, to brand her, more than he needed to breathe.

Backing her into the small bedroom, he kicked the door shut and guided her toward the bed. He broke the kiss and grabbed the hem of her t-shirt, pulling it over her head. Unable to resist a few quick sucks, he palmed her breasts, bent his head, and sucked her nipples hard.

"Garek," Diane gasped, pushing his dark head into her chest. "Oh God, that feels so good."

His breathing heavy, Garek released her nipple with a

popping sound. His hands found her jeans and quickly discarded them, throwing them to the wayside. Once she stood before him naked, she frantically helped him out of his clothes.

"You're the sexiest woman alive, Diane," Garek rasped, his voice thick. He backed her toward the bed, coming down on top of her as she fell onto it. "I need you so damn bad."

He couldn't get inside her pussy fast enough. Settling himself between her thighs, Garek placed one palm on the side of her head and used the other hand to guide his rigid cock to her opening.

"Please make love to me," Diane whispered, her hand massaging his bicep. "I've been wanting you for years, Garek."

Garek couldn't conceal the surprise in his expression. His green eyes widened a fraction, then narrowed in arousal.

The head of his cock found her opening. Their gazes locked. Garek gritted his teeth as he pushed himself in her tight, wet cunt. Diane groaned, her back arching beneath him.

"I've wanted you for years, too," Garek hoarsely admitted. He seated himself on a matching groan, then began to sink in and out of her, deep, slow strokes that made his toes curl. Sweet Jesus, but her pussy felt impossibly better than he'd fantasized it would. "No woman has ever compared to you, Diane."

"Oh, Garek—"

Diane gasped as he picked up the pace, fucking her

with all the intense, animalistic energy he'd been stockpiling over the years. Garek was done talking and ready to be one with the only woman on earth who wielded emotional power over him.

He sank in and out of her, moaning as he gluttonously indulged in her tight cunt. Nipples stiff, her tits jiggled beneath him with every thrust, turning him on all the more. Sweat-soaked skin slapped against sweat-soaked skin. The sound of her pussy suctioning in his cock permeated the small room with every outstroke.

Garek's balls were so tight he knew that orgasm was imminent. He didn't want to come yet, not by a long shot. He wanted to fuck her for hours, but his arousal was too great.

His eyes closed tightly and his muscles tensed as he fought to hold back his climax. He rode her hard, ruthlessly pumping in and out of her, while she moaned and fucked him back.

"Diane."

He took her harder, impaling her with deep, possessive strokes. His arms tightened around her, hands coming up beneath her shoulders and fingers digging into the flesh there. Garek didn't want to ever let her go.

One way or another, he'd make certain he didn't have to.

"I'm coming, Garek," she moaned, her voice thick. Her fingernails raked his back, mixing pleasure and pain. *"Now."*

"Me, too," he growled, guttural sounds emitting from his throat. He fucked her harder, faster, deeper, over and over, again and again. The scent of her arousal reached his nostrils, making them flare.

"Oh shit—*Diane.*"

Garek came on a loud roar, a sound of completion and dominance that reverberated through his body. Diane groaned out her orgasm, her pussy muscles contracting around his stiff flesh.

He continued to stroke in and out of her, and she continued to meet his thrusts. He kept up the frenzied pace until she'd milked every drop of cum out of him and, exhausted, he collapsed on top of her.

"Diane," Garek murmured, his voice hoarse with fatigue. He bent his neck and kissed her forehead. "Diane, thank you."

She smiled up at him, a lazy grin that told him she was a woman who had been well-loved. "Kiss me," she whispered, her eyes searching his.

Garek happily answered her request. He kissed her like she'd never been kissed before—like he'd never kissed a woman before.

I'm falling in love with you all over again, Diane.

Garek sighed and held her close, hoping that one day she would need him as much as he needed her.

Chapter 9

"Mr. Ennis, I fear that I do not understand what it is you want from me." Heinzman splayed his cultured, effeminate hands across the cherry desk in his office. "Ms. Sullivan and I struck a deal, you see." He lit a cigarette and slowly exhaled, his gaze boring into Garek's. "And I don't like losing money."

Garek frowned. The little worm was letting him know in so many words that if he planned to get Diane out of having to work the remainder of the cruise, he would be paying the scum a lot of money for it.

It didn't matter. This cruise was hard on Diane and her peace of mind was more than worth it.

Not that Garek didn't also harbor less than altruistic reasons for doing this. He couldn't stand other men seeing Diane naked, let alone touching the woman he considered to be his. Nevertheless, for once in his life it wasn't his own comfort he was thinking about, but someone else's. Diane hated this damn boat and he wanted to get her off it.

"How much do you want?" Garek murmured, coming straight to the point.

Heinzman had the gall to look surprised. "I don't understand—"

"Yes, you do." Garek grunted, his gaze narrowing at his adversary. "Name your price and quit wasting my time."

The faux astonishment quickly melted away. "Twenty-five thousand euros for all my trouble." His caterpillarlike eyebrows slowly inched up. "And Ms. Sullivan is free to go without having to pay me back."

He had expected the slimeball to go for fifty. Twenty-five was no problem. "Done."

When Garek had informed his best friend this morning of his intention to rescue Diane, so to speak, he had expected Rodney to look at him like he'd gone crazy. Rodney hadn't. Nor had he asked for an explanation. That was just as well because Garek hadn't been up for providing one. He was still weighing his feelings and figuring things out.

He felt intense emotions where Diane Sullivan was concerned, always had. He just didn't know what to label them. On one hand, it seemed absurd to call yourself in love with a woman you hadn't seen in sixteen years, but on the other hand, the feelings were still there.

Garek rose from his chair and turned to leave, but not

before throwing Heinzman one last frown. "I'll settle our bill before I leave the ship," he muttered.

He would leave *The Carnal Voyage* today—with Diane. He blew out a breath, hoping he wasn't presumptuous in assuming she wanted to be rescued.

Where is he?

Diane hadn't seen heads nor tails of Garek since they'd made love last night—the single most incredible experience of her life outside of giving birth to Jenna.

When she awoke this morning, Garek had already been gone. The note he left behind was brief, but sweet:

> *I went to take care of a few things, didn't have the heart to wake you. Sleep well, gorgeous, and I'll see you later.*
> *Garek xo*

She knew it was totally adolescent, but she couldn't get the "xo" he'd signed on the note out of her head. It wasn't quite an I-love-you, but it was still pretty heady.

It's been hours since I woke up. If he plans to come back, then where is he?

She hesitated. Maybe that note had been the Garek Ennis equivalent to the old "I'll call you" line.

Her heart sank. "Forget it, Cinderella," Diane muttered as she harshly set down two beers on a serving tray. The yellow, frothy liquid spilled off over the sides of the glasses. "The ball is over and it's time to go back to waiting tables."

It was now day four. Three more days to go and the nightmare of a cruise would end. Of course, she thought dejectedly, contact with Garek would end, too.

Spending time with him in Gouda had been great. Making love to him had been beyond wonderful. It was as if the sixteen years of separation had melted away and she was back in high school again, daydreaming about Garek falling in love with her while she doodled in her notebook during English Lit. She just prayed this encounter didn't end like the ones in high school had, with nothing positive coming of it.

Where are you, Garek?

Diane worried with her bottom lip. Maybe she had bored him. Such a possibility was painfully plausible. She was just simple, old Diane, not one of the worldly, sophisticated types Garek was accustomed to spending his time with.

That thought shouldn't matter, but it did. Still, she knew she'd carry on with life no matter what curveballs it threw her.

The boat had docked an hour ago in Delft, a town in the Netherlands. Perhaps Garek had decided to join the off-boat excursion, this time without her.

Diane told herself to stop behaving like an idiot. She sighed, telling herself to let it go. There had been no sense

in crying over Garek in high school, but she had. She refused to do the same thing as a grown woman, if even just
proverbially.

"Ms. Sullivan."

Diane started at the sound of the unfamiliar voice.
Wide-eyed, she whirled around with the tray in her hands,
more beer spilling out of the glasses. She had never spoken
to the man before, but she recognized him as one of the
ship's security personnel.

She softly cleared her throat. Her gaze raked over the
big, blond German man. "How can I help you?"

"I'm afraid you need to come with me."

Her forehead wrinkled. His accent was thick—perhaps
she had misunderstood him. "I'm sorry?"

"Put down the tray and follow me."

Diane blinked, uncertain of what was going on. She did
as the security guard requested, though, and trailed him
from the dining car. As she was leaving she noticed another
nude female worker entering. Had she been reassigned
again? Good grief, she hoped not! Naked waitressing was
enough of an ordeal without adding new, seedier ingredi-
ents into the mix.

"Can you tell me what this is about?" Diane asked,
walking quickly to keep up with him. Her breasts jiggled
with the brisk gait. "I feel the most comfortable working in
the dining car."

The big German didn't pause in his stride. "You aren't
working anywhere," he muttered, leading her toward a

small room off the boat's central kitchen. When she entered it, she immediately noticed her valise set on a chair. Someone had packed her clothes—probably him—and brought the trunk here. "Put on something to wear and I will escort you off the ship."

Her eyes widened and her mouth worked up and down, but nothing came out. Unable to effectively respond, Diane watched the security agent leave the room and shut the door behind him.

Her pulse picked up, adrenaline racing through her system. Heinzman had fired her? Oh, no! She *had* to talk to him. She couldn't afford to pay him back the ten thousand dollars!

A part of Diane was relieved, but the realistic part was concerned. Ten thousand dollars was a lot of money to owe someone, especially so for a single mom. It would take her half of forever to come up with that kind of money without starving herself in the process.

"I'll just have to raise the cash," Diane told herself as she threw on a bra and panties. She nodded definitively, telling herself she could do it. "At least I don't have to endure another moment of this awful ship."

The plane ticket was in her name. She wouldn't have to figure out an alternate way to get home. She would, however, have to pay the airline a penalty for changing her ticket and leaving the Netherlands early. She didn't have much cash left on her debit card, but she had enough to pay the fine and return to Ohio.

That knowledge having firmly taken root, relief at leaving three days early washed through Diane. A big weight lifted off her shoulders as she slid into one of her many cotton sundresses, this one a pale blue to match her eyes. Slipping into her sandals, she picked up her valise and all but threw open the door.

"I'm ready," Diane announced, smiling like a simpleton. The security agent raised an eyebrow at her obvious joy, but said nothing. "You will escort me off the boat now?"

"Yes." He cleared his throat, then motioned for her to follow him. "You have my apologies, Ms. Sullivan. I do not enjoy this task."

It was more than fine by her. "Everything's okay. I understand."

"Mr. Ennis was very specific, you see. You are to be removed from *The Carnal Voyage* immediately."

Diane's smile faded. Her heart dropped into her stomach. "I'm sorry?"

The security agent ignored her, as if he realized that he'd said too much. Diane followed him in silence, the skip no longer a part of her walk. Garek didn't have to go to such great lengths to avoid her. If he didn't want her around all he had to do was say so.

Relief at leaving early was displaced by anger and hurt. How could he do this to her knowing that she needed that ten thousand dollars? Had she misjudged him *that* badly?

When at last they were on land, Diane turned to the security agent with a sigh. "Tell Heinzman I'll pay him back as soon as I possibly can. It might take a few years, but I'll do it."

The agent's forehead wrinkled. "Pay him back?"

"The ten thousand dollars."

He waved that away. "You owe him nothing. Have a safe journey home, Ms. Sullivan."

Another bout of relief, this one all but knocking her to her knees. Heinzman didn't expect her to pay him back? She considered that for a moment, then realized she shouldn't have to anyway. She hadn't been fired for dereliction of duty, but because Garek Ennis wanted her gone.

"Thank you," Diane said quietly. She took a deep breath and slowly exhaled. It was time to put the past behind her and start anew. "Goodbye."

"You *what?*"

Garek's face mottled red with fury as he stared down Heinzman from the other side of his desk. He had decided to go find the little sewer rat when Diane failed to meet him in his stateroom per his instructions to Heinzman.

They were supposed to leave the boat together. Diane was not supposed to be "escorted" off it. If she knew Garek had something to do with it, she'd never forgive him. At least if they left together he could explain his intentions.

"I had her removed from the boat," Heinzman mumbled, his normally pompous expression taking on an alarmed note. "Perhaps I should have consulted you—"

It was the last thing Heinzman said before Garek punched him square in the jaw. Enraged, and more than a little worried about Diane, Garek stopped himself from injuring the asshole further and prowled from the office.

Chapter 10

The longer Diane walked the streets of Delft, the better she felt. Her deflated spirits slowly lifted, replacing the earlier turmoil with calm acceptance. Like a slave released from bondage, Diane felt the chains of sexual oppression lifted from her shoulders.

The only thing that still saddened her was the meanness with which Garek had forced her from his life. He could have simply told her he didn't want to see her, but instead he chose the coward's way out.

He had hurt her, the very thing she'd feared would come to pass. Still, Diane would have been lying if she said she regretted making love to Garek, because she didn't. In his mind, she was probably just another fuck, but in hers it had meant so much more than that.

Diane wound her way back to *De Grutto Haus*, a cute little alehouse where she'd found a cheap, clean room to sleep in until her plane left in three days. The owners—an older couple—had even offered to drive her to the airport. Luck had been smiling on Diane when she'd wandered into the pub, for the airline didn't have any seats available on an earlier flight.

She was glad it worked out this way. They were charging her far less for the room than the change penalty for the airline ticket would have been. Plus, she had the added bonus of experiencing another foreign city.

The outside of the two-hundred-year-old structure had been freshly painted blue and yellow. The colors of the buildings were all so vivid and lively, but Diane had taken an instant liking to *De Grutto Haus*.

A frown marred Diane's face as a far-off sound caught her ears. What was that noise? It almost sounded as though someone was calling her name.

Turning around in front of the alehouse, Diane's blue eyes widened as she saw Garek waving at her from a distance, her name roaring from his lips. Heart thumping wildly, she whirled around, not bothering to look back.

He'd done enough. Apparently he didn't know when to stop.

Diane's first thought was to disappear into the pub and up to her room. If she did that, however, Garek would know where to find her. He might cause a scene and embarrass her in front of the people who had shown her such kindness.

Her pulse skyrocketing, Diane took off walking. She briskly made her way into a narrow alley beside the alehouse, uncertain of where she should go. The hurt returned and all she could think about was putting as much distance between them as possible.

"Diane!" Garek bellowed. She could hear him running to catch up with her. "Diane, please let me explain!"

She stopped in her tracks and spun around to face him. Nostrils flaring, she balled her fists at her sides. "Explain what?" Diane asked, angry and upset. "Explain that you didn't possess the courage to tell me goodbye yourself so you had me thrown off the boat?"

"That's not true," Garek panted, nearing her. She could tell his knee was troubling him and struggled not to care. "It didn't happen like that. I swear it. Please, baby," he said. "Just let me explain."

She wanted so badly to believe him. She just prayed whatever it was he had to say rang true. "You've got my attention," she said, doing her best to sound cold, while feeling hopelessly hurt on the inside. "Say whatever it is you have to say."

Garek wasted no time in telling her exactly what had happened. Diane's shoulders slumped with relief, emotions—good ones this time—taking their toll on her.

"Are you mad, baby?" Garek softly asked. "Maybe you didn't need rescuing. Hell, you've made it all these years just fine without me and—"

Diane threw her arms around him and kissed him with

all the passion she harbored inside. He growled, then kissed her back, his strong arms protectively wrapped around her.

"Did you really punch him?" Diane asked, breaking the kiss.

"Damn straight." Garek's heart was in his eyes. "I don't play when it comes to you. Never have, and never will."

Diane smiled. Her gaze found his. "I love you, Garek. I've always loved you."

He grunted, but held her close to him. "You'd better," Garek teasingly threatened her, his chin resting on her head, "because I love you, too, and you're stuck with me for life."

No better promise had ever been made in the history of promises. She grinned, and hugged him back tightly.

Diane Sullivan had come to Europe to make some money so life could begin anew. Fate had led her back right where she'd started long before L.A. had come calling.

Fate was taking her home. To Ohio, to Jenna, and to Garek.

NAUGHTY NANCY

A Trek Mi Q'an Tale

Congrats on finding your happy ending, Nancy.

Prologue

Nancy Lombardo bit down on her bottom lip as her eyes warily shifted toward the old woman. The crone had to be a witch, she thought. In a town like Salem, Massachusetts— and on Halloween night no less—she couldn't be anything but a witch.

Either that or an extremely-eccentric-looking-homeless-person-with-a-penchant-for-wearing-black-robes-and-loud-blue-eyeshadow-while-she-stood-there-stirring-only-God-knows-what-around-in-a-cauldron-as-she-chanted-in-what-sounded-to-be-Latin.

Nancy sighed. She really should have taken that job in Anchorage. The weirdest thing she would have had to worry about encountering in Alaska was getting kidnapped by a lonely mountain man who hadn't laid eyes on a woman since his inbred wife had passed on to—well, wherever it was inbred wives passed on to.

Nancy's back went ramrod straight as she continued walking down the dark alley. She refused to be afraid, she sniffed. This was her night, damn it. The night she was going to saunter into her friend Lori's party and shine like the belle of the ball.

No more wallflower Nancy. No more fat girl out. No more watching through the spectacles perched on the end of her nose as men looked past her to the dimwitted idiots standing behind her with the buff bodies and unbuff brains. Tonight *she* was going to be one of those dimwitted idiots with the buff bodies and the unbuff brains!

Well okay, so she wasn't exactly dim-witted. And her body wasn't exactly buff. And, she grimly conceded, she had graduated at the top of her class in law school.

Damn it!

" 'Tis naught tae worry aboot," the old woman croaked, causing Nancy to lose her train of thought.

"Huh?"

Nancy's gaze shot toward where the old woman had been stirring her cauldron—the very same black-clad figure who had been standing on the opposite side of the alley, but who had somehow managed to land directly in front of her.

"Goodness," she breathed out as her hand instinctively flew up to shield her heart, "you scared me."

The old woman's weathered face crinkled into what on

most people would be considered a smile. On her it looked more like a pasty slit in between a bunch of equally pasty, white wrinkles.

Nancy swallowed a bit nervously as she waited to see what the old woman wanted. She absently adjusted her Xena: Warrior Princess costume, shifting the sword belt to the side. She winced and moved it back. The tip of the sword kept poking through its scabbard and jabbing her in the thigh.

Damn it!

"Can I help you with something?" Nancy asked in clipped tones. Call her a tad on the defensive side, but it was Halloween night and the old woman gave her the creeps. She kept staring into her eyes as if searching for something, but otherwise the mysterious witch remained silent.

A suspended moment passed in eerie quiet as the two women locked eyes. It gave Nancy enough time to let the guilt settle in. She sighed.

"I didn't mean to yell at you," she said quietly, her expression apologetic. She smiled. "I guess we all get a little freaked out on a night like this."

She decided to ignore the fact that the old woman was the reason she was freaked out to begin with.

" 'Twill be a long journey," the old witch murmured. Her palm came up and rested on Nancy's forehead as she continued to study her face. "But 'twill be worth the sacrifices when all is said and done. And love shall be yers."

Nancy's eyes darted back and forth as the old woman began to chant. She prayed nobody walked by and saw this!

Back in law school Nancy had been taught how to effectively deal with many different types of bizarre situations, but this one had definitely not been covered in any of the college texts. When the old woman's chanting picked up to a fevered squeal akin to the sound of a pig being slaughtered for Sunday dinner, she felt her cheeks redden.

Nope, definitely not covered in the law school texts.

Damn it!

"Are you okay?" Nancy bit out. She tried to politely remove the old crone's palm from her forehead, but the wrinkled thing wouldn't budge. She absently wondered if the old woman had been an arm wrestler in her heyday. "Do you need an aspirin or something?" Her tongue darted out to wet her lips as the squealing grew shriller. "I think I have a stick of gum tucked away in my scabbard if you—"

Nancy blinked. Her breath caught in the back of her throat.

The old woman was gone.

"Good grief," she mumbled as her head darted back and forth. "Where did she go?"

After a suspended moment just standing there with her mouth agape—no doubt looking like the village idiot—she shook her head and sighed. She really should have taken that job in Anchorage.

Regally straightening her back, Nancy dismissed the oddity of the situation from her mind and continued to walk down the dark alley. She could hear music and laughter floating out of a window a ways down, which could only mean she was almost at the old warehouse Lori had renovated for tonight's Halloween party.

Nancy took a deep breath as she wondered for the fiftieth time since she'd left her apartment an hour ago what everyone would think of her new look. Not the Xena costume itself, but the bodily changes that had gone along with it. During her two-month leave of absence from the law firm, she had used the time to completely transform her image.

Gone was the schoolmarm bun she had always tightly wrapped her hair into and in its place was a sultry mane of light brown cascading hair, to which her stylist had thoughtfully added golden highlights. Gone was the spinsterish pair of oversized spectacles that had sat suspended on the tip of her nose, replaced by a pair of translucent contact lenses that showed off the rich chocolate brown of her eyes.

And, she thought with much relief, gone were those extra forty pounds of bulk. In their place was a voluptuous form that was beginning to show the first signs of muscle tone from daily exercise and sensible eating. She wasn't skinny, and knew she never would be; in fact, she was still somewhat fleshy, but for the first time in years she looked and felt healthy.

The Xena outfit was more than a costume to her, she realized. It was the very symbol of the new Nancy Lombardo, a Nancy Lombardo who was no longer content to sit on the sidelines as a passive spectator while life passed her by. She was an alpha female now. A warrior woman.

A warrior woman who hadn't had sex since three presidents ago.

Damn it!

But that pitiful circumstance would change tonight, she reassured herself as she straightened her shoulders and walked determinedly up the back steps that would take her to the renovated warehouse loft above. Times were changing. The wallflower had died. The warrior woman within had awoken. She was a phoenix rising up from the flames of abject grief and despair. She was—

Bah! Times were changing. Enough said.

Nancy took a calming breath as she pushed open the warehouse doors and strolled inside. She instantly forgot her nervousness as she glanced around, the smile on her face indicative of her festive mood. The old Stapleton warehouse looked great.

Lori had decorated the place perfectly, the dark atmosphere with the scattered lights of jack-o-lanterns setting just the right mood. Skeletons stood across the room at either side of the buffet table, ghoulishly guarding the different sweets and appetizers that had been set out for the hungry guests. The music playing in the background had a New Age, Gothic feel to it. She loved it. The old warehouse looked perfect.

"Nancy! Is that you? Wow!"

Nancy's head snapped to attention as a beautiful, vivacious redhead strolled up to her side. She smiled. Lori looked great tonight dressed in a slinky little witch's get-up that emphasized the curviness of her body. "Yep, it's me," she said on a grin. "How's life in your dad's manufacturing business treating you these days?"

Lori groaned as she rolled her eyes. "Busy. I even have to work later on tonight if you can believe it."

"On Halloween? You're kidding!"

"Afraid not."

"You're not staying at your own party then?"

Lori embraced her in a hug, her smile full of welcome and admiration. They hadn't seen each other in two months and it did Nancy's ego some good to realize her friend liked the changes she saw.

"I'll be here for another hour or so, but I have to cut out early." Lori sighed. "I've been looking forward to this party since last year's, but I promised my father I'd take care of a few business matters for him."

"How exciting," Nancy said dryly.

"Exactly." Lori grinned. "But enough of me—look at you! Nancy you look head-to-toe terrific."

Unaccustomed to compliments of a physical nature, Nancy found herself blushing. "Thank you."

Lori patted her on the shoulder. "Go mingle while I use the little witch's room. I'll be right back."

"Will do."

After Lori left her side, Nancy took her first thorough look around at the other invited guests. To her utter amazement and delight, she found more than one pair of male eyes flicking over her new form and checking her out. Flustered by the attention, and as unused to it as she was to verbal compliments, she nervously lifted her hand to push the spectacles up the bridge of her nose—only to realize halfway there that she wasn't wearing any.

Damn it!

She took a deep breath. She could do this. She could mingle with the male guests and behave as naturally in a social setting as any other woman would. She was more than a woman, she reminded herself. She was a warrior woman. Xena. Phoenix from the—

Bah! She could do this. Enough said.

Her chin going up a notch, Nancy firmly told herself that she would—right now at this very moment in time—join the party and seek out an attractive male to talk to. A simple thing to most women, perhaps, but a portentous symbol to herself.

Taking what felt like her millionth calming breath of the evening, Nancy adjusted her sword belt and resumed her stroll through the throng of guests.

Tonight, she would get a life. Tonight, she would find a man. Tonight, she would end the bitter solitude of not having known a man's bed since big hair had been in fashion. Tonight, she would—

Bah! She would get some cock tonight if it killed her. Enough said.

Chapter 1

6067 Y.Y. (Yessat years)
Hunting Grounds of the F'al Vader Pack Planet Khan-Gor
("Planet of the Predators") Seventh Dimension

"Ahhh . . . CHOO!"

Nancy's eyes squinted shut as her entire body shuddered from the violence of her sneeze. She sneezed three times more in rapid succession, then waved her hands madly about to clear the puff of whitish smoke that was swirling around her like a cranky cloud.

Good grief. What weird concoction had that old witch blown at her? It was translucent white and very sticky, much like a resin.

Nancy harrumphed as she absently studied her hands. She never should have decided to take a break from Lori's party. She never should have exited to the back alley in order to regain her composure. So what if a man had engaged her in conversation, she thought acidly. Any *normal* woman would have been able to sustain a casual conversation with a man without finding it necessary to take a break and air herself out before resuming said conversation.

Damn it!

Nancy's lips pinched together. Perhaps she really should have taken that job in Alaska. She doubted she would have gotten so fidgety around a mountain man. She doubted she would have cared whether or not such a male found her impressive enough to seduce. Her biggest concern with impressing a mountain man would have been whether or not she looked inbred enough to suit his sexual taste.

Nancy's back went ramrod straight. This was enough mental babbling, she babbled to herself. She'd gotten her air, as well as some weird, sticky white junk blown at her by the feisty old witch, so it was time to go back inside and continue the conversation she'd been having but minutes prior with Justin.

Justin seemed like a good enough guy, she assured herself. He wasn't an athletic hunk by any stretch of the imagination, but then again she doubted *Playboy* would be contacting her any time soon, begging her to pose for a centerfold spread.

Nancy supposed that if she possessed a body worthy of *Playboy*, she probably wouldn't be so damned unsure of herself where the opposite sex was concerned. But she didn't, and she was. She'd just have to figure out a way to get over it.

One thing was for certain, she thought as she finished clearing the air of the whitish smoke with her hands, her goal of getting laid tonight would be a hell of a lot easier to accomplish if Justin were a more forceful type. As it was she felt as if she was the one doing all the seducing—hardly an easy feat for a woman who'd been known as a reclusive social mouse not even a full day ago.

Nancy took a deep breath as she squared her shoulders. It was time to go back inside. It was time to rejoin the party. It was time to seduce the hell out of nerdy, geeky Justin. She was a warrior woman now, she reminded herself with a sniff. Xena. Phoenix from the—

Bah! She was going to fuck that little dweeb tonight if it was the last thing she ever did. Enough said.

Her chin went up a notch. Her nostrils flared. She was determined, damn it. Horny and determined. She hadn't purchased those condoms tucked away in her scabbard for nothing.

Gritting her teeth, she took a resolute step toward the backdoor entrance to Lori's party. Warrior woman, she silently reiterated as her nostrils flared impossibly farther. Alpha female, she grunted, her muscles flexing.

It was time to go back inside. It was time to rejoin the party. It was time to—

She stilled. It was time to figure out where in the hell she was.

"Oh, shit."

Nancy's jaw dropped open as the air finally cleared of the whitish smoke and she got her first unimpeded look at her surroundings. Her eyes widened and her teeth clicked

shut as it dawned on her that she was standing in some sort
of . . .

Nest?

"What the hell?" she muttered.

Nancy gaped down at her feet, noting that the structure
she was standing in was silver and glittery, the fabric similar
to that of twined tree bark. Worse yet, there were animal
pelts scattered all about the nest, as if it had been recently
occupied.

She gulped. If the nest had been recently engaged, it
didn't take an Einstein to figure out that whatever had occupied it would probably come back. And it might not like
to share.

Shit. Shit. Shit.

Her heart pounding, Nancy quickly made her way to the
other side of the silver nest. The shell swayed a bit, scaring
the daylights out of her. She immediately came to a stand-
still. Waiting for a moment to find her nerve, she crept
slowly to the side, careful not to rock the glittery thing in the
process.

She blew out a breath. In the befitting words of
SpongeBob SquarePants, holy mother of pearl.

Nancy understood that she was in shock. Breathing was
difficult—hell, even blinking was difficult. She had no idea
where she was or how she had gotten here but—

"Oh—my—God."

Standing by one wall of the nest, Nancy's entire body
froze in place when she glanced to the terrain that sur-

rounded it. Or more to the point, when she glanced to the terrain that *didn't* surround it.

"I am in a damn tree," she said in a monotone. She was so shocked she couldn't even blink. "The witch actually put me in a tree."

Insomuch as she could tell, there was no land on any side of the nest to step off onto. It appeared to be high up—very, very high up, she uneasily noted. The silver nest was perched in a tree and surrounded on all sides by a towering view of a silvery, icy mountainscape hundreds of feet below it.

Her heart rate soared. Silver-ice mountains? Hundreds of feet *below* her?

What a damn day!

She gulped. Nancy'd always been afraid of heights. The nest she was currently standing in was up higher than she'd ever been before. If she couldn't see any land directly below the nest, then that could only mean that—

She gasped, noting for the first time that a pointed piece of silver ice jutted up from the middle of the nest. That could only mean that—

She swallowed roughly.

That could only mean that the nest was impaled upon a narrow, pointed piece of icecap. One singular piece of ice was all that held the nest up, she thought hysterically. It was all that stood between keeping the nest perched upright on the mountain apex and allowing the nest to plummet only God knows how far to the ground.

I'm going to kill that old witch!

Blood rushed to Nancy's head, pounded through her veins. Her heart rate accelerated impossibly higher as a near-maddening hysteria bubbled up inside of her. Her eyes wide with fright, she opened her mouth and did the only thing she could think to do in such a situation.

She screamed. Loudly.

"Help Meeeeeeeeeeeeeeeeeeee!"

She screamed out her platitude three times more, her voice hoarse when at last she stopped. Panting for air, she braved another glance over the ledge, immediately noting that the plummet from up in the nest didn't look any more welcoming than it had before she'd started wailing like a banshee.

For as far as the eye could see there was nothing but mountains and silver ice. The ice was everywhere, coated everything, and formed slick shields on mountains that were so tall she couldn't see their bottoms.

"What—is—going—on?" she bit out.

People didn't just walk into an alley and land in another world! She *had* to be hallucinating. She didn't do drugs and wasn't much for drinking. The only thing Nancy could figure was her mind had somehow snapped.

I'm going to die! And just when I finally had a half-assed presentable body!

A gust of icy wind hit her in the face, inducing Nancy to realize for the first time just how cold it was up here— wherever up here was. Shivering, she raised her hands and began to briskly rub them up and down her arms, absently working the chill bumps out of her flesh while simultaneously racking her brain for a way out of her predicament.

She bit her lip. She was up in a nest. The nest was perched on top of one of those pointed mountain apexes she'd just seen below. How would she ever get out of here? And when—and if—she did get out, where to then?

Her nostrils flared to wicked proportions. Alaska. Why the hell hadn't she taken that job in Alaska? "Damn old witch," she mumbled under her breath. "I should never have given her my last stick of gum. I should have . . ."

She didn't know why, couldn't say what premonition it was that instructed her to shut up and look down, but slowly, ever so slowly, Nancy's gaze trailed down her body until she ascertained that—

Yep, she was butt naked.

Damn it!

Ooooh, she thought angrily, her lips forming a snarl, the witch had gone too far this time. Not only was she stuck in a silvery glitter nest made of twined bark, not only was the nest thousands of feet off the nearest ground, not only was her body covered in a sticky white residue, not only was it colder than she didn't know what up here, but she was also naked. Butt naked.

Her hands fisted into tight balls and fell to her sides. When she got out of this place—and she *would* get out of it—she was going to strangle that old witch and enjoy the depraved activity with every cell of her being.

So *this* is the thanks she was to receive for being kind to that woman, she thought melodramatically. She couldn't believe this was her reward for being nice enough to give the old woman the last stick of gum she'd had on her, the very one she'd tucked away in her—

"Scabbard."

Nancy let out a breath of relief when she realized she might be naked, but she still had her sword and scabbard with her. She didn't know why that knowledge gave her such comfort, but it did.

Perhaps it was because the sword, at present, was the only connection she had to the world she'd been transported from. Perhaps it was because the sword—useless as it no doubt was since she didn't know how to use it—would still offer her minimal protection from any predator that might think to reclaim its nest while she was occupying it. Whatever the reason, it did the trick and helped her to calm down a bit.

"I have to get out of here," she murmured, her brown eyes darting warily back and forth.

Just then another gust of chillingly cold wind slammed into her face, making her flesh goosebump. Her teeth chattering, she sank slowly to her knees and ran her hands over one of the animal pelts lining the nest. It was warm and fuzzy, and very inviting at the moment.

As she looked around she noted that the sun was rapidly fading and that darkness would soon overtake this mountain she was stranded atop. The darkness, she thought nervously, would cause the temperature to plummet even lower.

She spent a threadbare moment considering her options, but realized rather quickly that she didn't have any to consider. There was no getting off this mountaintop without aid. She would have to bide her time and pray that the old witch decided to poof her back to Salem in the morning.

Climbing under the intoxicatingly warm animal pelts, Nancy expelled a deep breath as she fell asleep with her sword laid against her backside. It was there, the still-warm metal reassuringly within reaching distance if she needed it.

Drowsy, confused, angry, but mostly frightened, Nancy allowed herself to succumb to slumber. She hoped against hope that she was already asleep and would wake up to find that all of this had been no more than a bad dream.

When her gaze flicked up and she took notice of four crimson full moons tinting the nighttime sky atop the mountain a haunting blood red, she closed her eyes and told herself it simply had to be a dream.

A very horrific, intensely frightening, could-drive-a-woman-to-drink, bad dream.

Damn it!

Chapter 2

Vorik F'al Vader, the eldest of seven sons and heir to his sire Yorin's dominion, landed silently on the ground, careful to make not a sound. He shape-shifted immediately from his winged *kor-tar* form and landed on humanoid feet, his heavily muscled body nigh unto naked, save the kilt wrapped about his waist and the pair of knee-high silver *muu* hide boots he wore.

Slowly, his dark-haired head came up, his acute silver gaze scanning the mountainside for any sign of *yenni* movement. He felt the excitement of the hunt coursing through his veins, knowing 'twas at long last time to round up his own pen of pets. Some would be bartered at market, aye, but most he would keep for himself.

What made a yenni so valuable was not only the she-beast's insatiable hunger for humanoid male seed, but 'twas also the sheer beauty of her fertile form—the fleshiness of her hips, the milkiness of her pale skin, the way she'd daintily flick her tail about whilst she suckled seed from a Khan-Gori male's cock.

Vorik sighed a bit dreamily, and with much anticipation. He had seen eighteen Yessat years as of this moon-rising, so now 'twas his rite of passage into manhood to take as many yenni as he desired into his keeping—and into his bedfurs.

For years he had fantasized about what it might feel like to have a hoard of females suckle from him, drink from him, feed from him. He would care for them well, he knew, making himself and his cock ever available to see to their feminine appetites.

He was a selfless barbarian, he told himself with a sniff. No matter how much seed his pets would wish to suckle from him, he'd see to it he provided them with it. Aye, he was forever putting the needs of others before his own. He was forever thinking of the happiness of other creatures before he saw fit to care for himself. He was forever—

Bah! He wished to have his cock suckled til 'twas possible it fell off. Enough said.

Vorik took a deep breath and closed his eyes, drinking crisp cold air into his lungs. He needed to calm himself, he knew, for his man sac was already tight and nigh unto bursting just thinking about the hunting booty that would soon be his. 'Twas cruel indeed the ancient custom that forbade a Khan-Gori male to lose his virginity until he saw eighteen Yessat years, for it seemed that his cock and man sac had been in desperate need of satiation ever since the moon-rising he'd turned twelve.

Every waking moment for the past six years had been hellish, every hour had passed as an eternity. The need to thrust into the warm, suctioning flesh of his destined mate had come upon him at hourly intervals, nigh unto driving him insane.

Because the males of his species realized they weren't likely to find their Bloodmates until much later in life, if at all, 'twas the way of it on Khan-Gor to expend one's seed within the bodies of the dim-witted yenni until at which time a Bloodmate was claimed. Even then a Khan-Gori male was expected to keep up the feeding of his pets until they were bartered at market, for 'twould be cruel indeed to allow the beautiful creatures to slowly starve to death.

Vorik harrumphed. He could never be so cruel.

As is ever the way of nature, the system worked out just fine, for female yenni could not survive without feeding on seed. And so it came to pass through the perfection of trillions of Yessat years of evolution that the yenni provided sticky flesh to thrust into and voracious mouths to suckle with whilst the Khan-Gori male provided his dim-witted pet with food. 'Twas a perfect system. Or, Vorik mentally qualified as his lips turned down grimly, mayhap it would have been a perfect system had he been allowed to indulge of yenni from his twelfth year onward.

By the tit of the she-god, he needed a suckling.

A soft purring sound a mile away snagged Vorik's attention, inducing him to smile slowly. He had heard that very sound many a time emitting from the pen his sire's yenni were caged in. The sound always meant one of two things—the yenni had either fallen asleep after feeding well, or she was cleaning herself.

His nostrils flared as he breathed in the scent of her. It mattered not that she was a mile off in distance, for the males of his species had the most acute sensory systems of any known creature in the seventh dimension of time and space. He could smell her skin, could smell her pussy, could smell the scent of her arousal.

Fangs exploded into Vorik's mouth as he shape-shifted back into his kor-tar form. Faster than an eye can blink, his skin dimmed from its usual golden bronze color to a translucent shade of silver ice. Talons that tore prey apart so easily spiked out from where his toes had been, and wings that spanned twelve feet across protruded from his back as he leapt skyward and took flight.

At last, he thought as his manhood hardened, *oh, aye, at last.*

He tracked her easily, a skill any Khan-Gori male perfected by childhood. Part and parcel of growing into manhood on his planet was learning to provide food for one's family, and one could not provide food for his pack without a hunter's skill at taking down living, moving prey. This yenni would provide him with no food, 'twas true, for 'twould be Vorik who provided her with much nourishment.

Oh, aye.

He found the yenni cleaning herself near unto an ice-coated stream, her face lowered betwixt her thighs and her tongue darting out to lap at her own pussy. Vorik's nostrils flared as he watched her, her pink tongue meticulously rimming the folds of her flesh, then darting up on a purr to lick at the bud nestled between the lips. She purred and cooed as she lapped at herself, and Vorik found himself simply staring at the beauty of the scene.

This yenni female was nigh unto perfect in her beauty. Her creamy breasts were large, the pink nipples that capped them round and full. Her hair was long and dark, and looked soft to the touch. The only aspect of the she-beast he found to be a turn-off was the thinness of her form. 'Twas obvious she was no alpha female, for a dominant she-beast would better know how to feed on male seed.

Well, Vorik grunted, verily it mattered not, for he would teach the she-beast whatever lessons she needed to learn in the art of feeding. 'Twould be ideal if she already knew what she was about, but such was apparently not the way of it. Ah well, no matter how many sucklings it took to teach her how to get great spurts of seed in one feeding, he would be patient and understanding in waiting for her to catch on.

By the tit of the she-god, he grumbled as he licked his fangs, he prayed she was as dim-witted as she looked.

Vorik's cock stiffened whilst he landed on his feet and shape-shifted into his humanoid form. His fangs retreated, and his wings and talons seemingly disappeared, as he silently made his way through the thick of the trees to stalk and capture the yenni by the stream. He was careful to make not a sound as he prowled toward the open savannah from the forest, no cracking of ice under his feet, no rustling of branches overhead.

"Help Meeeeeeeeeeeeeeeeeeee?"

Vorik's entire body stilled as the feeding call of an alpha female yenni reached his ears. The shrill cry of the dominant female caused the yenni he'd been tracking but moments prior to whimper and scamper away, and he found himself uncaring of the fact that he'd just been thwarted of his hunting booty. He was intrigued indeed by this unexpected happening.

Verily, 'twas hard to stalk an alpha female. 'Twas even harder to track one who sounded to be desperately hungry, for they tended to stay well-fed. Mayhap, he thought to himself, she had followed a Khan-Gori predator to a hunting perch in the hopes of getting a meal and had managed to snare herself into a nest from which she could not escape in the doing.

"Help Meeeeeeeeeeeeeeeeeeeee! Help Meeeeeeeeeeeeeeeeeeeee! Help Meeeeeeeeeeeeeeeeeeeee!"

"Oh, aye," Vorik murmured, his man sac tightening. His acute silver gaze honed in on a mountain apex that looked to be a lengthy flight away. She was trapped all right—trapped and desperate to suckle a male nigh blind.

Vorik swallowed a bit roughly as he considered just how good of a suckling the dominant female was likely to give in her crazed, nigh unto starving state. Feeding her would like as naught kill him, for she would demand great spurts to sate her. His nostrils flared as he breathed in the crisp nighttime air.

By the tit of the she-god, he was ready to die.

Fangs exploded into Vorik's mouth once again as he shot up from the ground, his body transforming into his kor-tar form as he leapt upward.

He would find her in all haste.

He would feed her as any good master should.

He could not allow an alpha female to suffer from hunger pangs needlessly.

Ever thoughtful of others he was, he sniffed. Ever considerate of dim-witted creatures was he. Ever—

Bah! He wanted the she-beast to suck him dry. Enough said.

Chapter 3

Groggy with sleep, her eyelids firmly closed, Nancy's forehead wrinkled in incomprehension as she tried to figure out where the smooching sound she heard was coming from. It was a vaguely familiar noise, the type of kissy-fish lips, "here girl" sound a person would make if they were calling a dog over to them.

Her eyebrows shot up as she continued to sleep. Weird.

The sound was so bizarre to her, in fact, so misplaced, that she rolled over onto her side with a grumble, and fell back into a deep, snoring sleep within seconds, her long skinny sword pressed against her backside.

Moments later she felt a large palm settle on her belly, then reverently run over the excess flesh there. Even in her sleep, her lips pinched together in a frown as she groggily considered the fact that even two months of dieting and exercise hadn't been enough to get rid of her belly. Or her thighs. Or her butt.

Damn it!

The feel of a solid piece of warm flesh tapping against her lips induced Nancy's forehead to crinkle bewilderedly. The tapping, accompanied by the kissy-fish lips sound, was finally enough to rouse her from slumber and cause her eyelids to slowly flutter open.

Ooookay.

Nancy's eyes widened in shock as she gaped up at the huge man kneeling down beside her. She had never—*never*—seen a man so enormous as this one. His body, which looked ominously long even kneeling down, was so thick with muscle that she wouldn't have been surprised if he weighed in the vicinity of five hundred pounds. He wasn't burly or stocky in the slightest, for his musculature looked right on him, but he was incredibly big in every way.

Tap. Tap. Tap.

Tap—tap.

Tap—tap—tap—tap.

Tap.

"Whadddyaddnd." Unable to part her lips to speak without a surprise visitor sneaking inside, her nostrils flared as the big oaf continually tapped the head of his—extremely well-endowed!—penis against the swell of her lips. The gargantuan's own lips were still pursed in kissy-fish form as he slapped his manhood against her. The "here girl" sound he was emitting grew louder and more demanding.

The giant was treating her as if she were a dog and his penis a big bone to salivate over. She grunted. This was just too much.

Damn it!

What in the hell was going on? she mentally wailed. Who was this man? Where had that witch whisked her off to?

One thing was for certain, she hesitantly determined. She had never—not even once—seen a man so large as this one. She wasn't sure it was even genetically *possible* for a human male to be so gigantic.

Frightened, Nancy's eyes flew up to meet the giant's, the expression on her face indignant regardless to the scare he was giving her. Never show fear, she staunchly told herself, remembering what she'd once heard on an *Oprah* show about deterring a possible assailant. Never show fear.

Tap—tap—tap.

Tap—tap.

Tap—tap—tap.

Unfortunately, she grimly conceded as the head of his cock kept up its tempo against her lips, her lack of exhibited fear didn't seem to be impressing him all that much. And— eek!—she really wished he'd quit making that kissy-fish lips sound.

Damn it!

* * *

Vorik landed softly upon two feet in the Khan-Gori perch, shape-shifting into his humanoid form whilst he entered the nest. His fangs retreated, his eyes shifted back from red to silver, and the wings seemingly dissolved from his back as the beast submerged in favor of the man.

His breath caught when he saw her lying stretched out under animal hides in the middle of the nest, her saucy, silver, swordlike tail erect even whilst slumbering. There she was in all her suckling glory. The plump alpha female he'd tracked—and caught.

"Oh, aye, you like to feed," he murmured, his muscles clenching in anticipation as his gaze drank in her fertile form.

He bent down beside her, kneeling close to her slumbering body. He brushed off the animal pelts and ran a large hand over the soft skin of her full underbelly. She was fleshy, the dominant female was, and her love of eating was proof positive that she was to become a pet he would cherish and pamper for all time.

Vorik closed his eyes briefly and took a steadying breath. He was embarrassingly close to spurting before the yenni was even roused enough to suckle of him. His cock was as long and hard as 'twas possible for it to be and his man sac was so tight that the excruciatingly exquisite feeling bordered on pain.

Oh, aye.

His cock in hand, Vorik announced the arrival of a hearty meal to the dim-witted yenni by tapping the head of his staff against her lips, beckoning to her to eat. When her eyes fluttered open—by the ice of Mount Shalor they were beautiful!—he was certain 'twas the need of a meal he saw in her rounded gaze.

He tapped his cock harder against her mouth, nigh unto desperate for her suctioning lips to part. Sweat dotted his brow as he willed her mouth to open, as he prayed to the mating gods for surcease.

Oh, aye, he thought headily as his man sac tightened impossibly more, her nostrils were flaring, inhaling the scent of food no doubt. More aroused than he'd thought it possible for himself to become, his teeth gritted and his muscles clenched anticipatorily as he tapped his cock harder still against her lips.

She would part them eventually, he knew, for the lure of a hot meal would be too tempting to resist o'er long.

Vorik's eyes flicked over her fleshy underbelly, grazed over her full hips and breasts. Eventually the alpha female would part her suctioning lips.

And when she did, she would feed.

"Whaddydndg?" Nancy asked furiously, her lips firmly clamped shut. She ignored the heated stare his silver eyes gave back to her and, huffing, pushed his manhood away from her face as she came up on her knees. "What," she bit out, her teeth set, "are you doing?"

Oh no, she thought, her forcefulness wavering a bit.

His eyes—his damn eyes. They were . . . silver. Not gray, not light blue, not some murky could-be-human color, but sharp, piercing, acute . . . silver.

She gulped, scooting back a bit out of reflex.

The giant's breathing hitched just a little as his gaze meandered up and down her body. Naked on her knees before him, his piercing silver eyes seemed to meld as they flicked over her face, then down lower to her breasts, lower still to her tummy, and even lower yet to her—

"Shit," Nancy muttered, biting down on her lip. She backed up a bit more, scurrying away as quickly as one could while on their knees. She had forgotten she was naked. How could she have forgotten that?

Ggggggrrrrrr.

She gasped when the giant began to growl low in his throat, the sound he was emitting telling her without words that if she knew what was good for her, then she had best not move another inch away from him. Her jaw agape, her mind frenziedly trying to figure out a method of escape, she unthinkingly scooted farther away from him until she had all but trapped herself against the far wall of the nest.

"Oh my—eek!" Nancy's hands shot up to cover her ears as his low growl evolved into a blood-curdling roar of anger.

His eyes shifted from silver to dull-glowing crimson. Fangs exploded from his gums, exposing incisors long enough to tear her apart.

Her jaw came unhinged. Her hands fell down to her sides.

She really should have taken that job in Anchorage.

Silver eyes that turn red, Nancy thought in dawning horror, growls that become roars, fangs that . . . well . . . he had fangs!

Hysterically deciding she at last knew how Fay Wray felt when King Kong plucked her from the sacrificial altar on Skull Island, she backed up on her knees against the far wall of the nest. Her hands instinctively flew up to shield her ears once again. "Heeeelp mmmeeeeeeeeeeeeeee!"

Oddly, those shrieked out words seem to calm him, even satisfy him. "Huh?" Nancy's eyebrows shot up uncomprehendingly, wondering as she did why he'd had such a positive reaction to the shrill sound of her wailing.

The giant's eyes shifted back from crimson to silver, and his fangs retreated below the gumline as though they'd never been. The muscles in his huge—and naked!—body seemed to clench as he stood up . . . up . . . way up, and slowly inched his way toward her.

She harrumphed. He was grasping his penis by the base again and making those stupid kissy-fish noises as he arrogantly strode to stand before her kneeling form. He was beckoning to her again, calling out to her as though she were a dog and he was offering her a supreme cut of beef.

Damn it!

She swept a hand about grandly, purposely ignoring the horrific manner in which the nest was beginning to teeter back and forth. "Forget it," she sniffed. "It won't happen. Not now. Not—*eek!*"

Nancy screamed loud enough to wake the dead as the giant's added weight caused the nest to teeter too far to the side—far enough that she got a bone-chilling look at how far she'd be plummeting to her death if he came any closer. Her heart rate soared. Perspiration broke out all over her body.

"Okay!" she shrieked, her breasts heaving up and down. "You win! For the love of God you win, but please quit moving!"

Either he was purposely ignoring her words or he couldn't understand what she was saying, but either way the giant kept prowling toward her, cock in hand. Nancy panicked when she felt the nest sway down lower and, with a scream, lunged up at the colossal male. She jumped into his heavily muscled embrace, her only objective to keep him in the middle of the nest so that the structure would remain perched upright.

The giant laughed as he effortlessly caught her, dimples popping out on either cheek as he plucked her out of midair like a leaf. Nancy captured, he grinned down into her face.

Their eyes clashed. Her breath caught.

Damn he was handsome, Nancy thought rather warily, not at all liking the fact that her skin felt tingly and alive when it brushed up against the giant's. In fact, she felt more than alive and tingly—she felt downright turned on.

Huh?

Nancy chewed on her lower lip as she studied him, an

odd and completely out of place premonition that everything would be okay swamping her senses. He wouldn't
hurt her—not like that, not sexually. Her forehead crinkled
as she idly wondered how she could remain so calm and
sure given the situation. But there it was. She *was* sure.

And there was another feeling there as well, a gut instinct that shot through her and permeated every cell of her
consciousness as her brown eyes shot up once more to
meet his molten silver ones.

She gulped roughly. She wasn't certain how she knew,
didn't know what instinct or intuition was guiding her
thoughts, but she was sure of one thing: the witch didn't
plan to let her leave this place or this giant.

Ever.

Chapter 4

Nancy swallowed nervously as the giant laid her down on her back and settled his huge form next to hers. He curled his muscled body around her in such a way that her face was kept close to his swollen penis. Her breath came out in a rush, and she was surprised to find that her body was reacting fiercely to his.

But it wasn't the need to suck on him that was making her feel breathless and passionate, though she could ascertain that was precisely what the giant wanted from her. It was the need to mate with the huge predator that was arousing her so fiercely. She didn't just want to have sex with him, she thought uneasily. She wanted to actually mate with him, to have him implant his child in her womb.

"Oh lord," she whimpered, her nipples hardening, her

breath coming out in pants. She knew something wasn't right, wasn't as it should be. Human women do not react to human males like . . . like . . . good grief!—like dogs in heat. But that's exactly what she felt like, and what's worse, she could swear she felt every egg that lined her ovaries tingling, waiting to be fertilized.

Damn it!

Nancy groaned, clamping a hand to her forehead. What in the name of God was happening to her? Her lips formed a dramatic martyr's slash. What manner of species was this fanged predator that he could make her body react so damned primitively?

Her stomach rumbled, reminding her she hadn't eaten in ages. She'd been too keyed up at Lori's party to consume a morsel, and too worried about her waistline expanding to take a bite. But now—

Nancy's eyes flicked up to the giant's face as her breathing grew increasingly sporadic. Now, she thought worriedly as her eyes locked with his and she saw his breathing hitch, now she was suddenly hungry.

Vorik heard the yenni groan, the sound followed immediately by the noise of her empty belly rumbling.

Oh, aye, he thought shakily, his man sac tightening til 'twas nigh unto blue, at long last the alpha female was hungered enough to dine upon him. Every muscle in his body clenched in anticipation, and his breath came out in a rush. Her dim-witted eyes flew up to meet with his.

That an intelligence seemed to lurk behind the dominant female's gaze was of no interest to him at this juncture. All he could think on was the fact that after having been forced to wait so many agonizing years for bodily surcease, his cock was about to be suckled of seed.

He reached out and brushed a lock of hair away from her face. Verily, he had never seen hair the color of hers, a soft amber hue that made his heart ache.

The color of her bedamned hair made his heart ache? Arrg! By the tit of the she-god, he would not fall in love with a dim-witted yenni. Verily, he frowned, 'twould make him the laughingstock of his entire pack!

Vorik saw the hesitation in her eyes and wondered at it. Mayhap a former master had treated her badly, he thought sadly, his heart constricting yet further. His teeth gritted as he steeled himself against his emotions, yet he found that all the steeling in the galaxies could not keep his heart from thumping madly in tune with hers.

Ah well, no matter, he assured himself. 'Twas probably a normal reaction any male of his species had to the first pet he captured. Mayhap a barbarian always held a special place in his heart for the she-beast who becomes the first to suckle of him. 'Twas a passing fancy, that.

The heaving of her breasts caught his attention, inducing Vorik's hand to instinctively reach out and palm one.

'Twas large and full, he thought wonderingly, his breath hitching once more. He ran his thumb over the elongated rouge nipple. She gasped in pleasure. Vorik closed his eyes briefly whilst he dragged in a calming breath at the sound.

Her nipples were like *maji* fruits, he thought as his nostrils flared. Puffy at the base, long and ripe at the peak.

Vorik's silver eyes bore into the yenni's, the troubled look within her dark gaze still causing his heart to ache. He continued to stroke her silken mane of hair, his eyes gentling at her worried expression. His other hand reached further down her body until his thumb found her clit. He massaged it gently to soothe her. *"Sha nala faron, zya"* ['Twill be alright, little one]. He smiled softly. *"Khan-Gori m'alana fey"* [I will not harm you].

She looked as though she understood not what his words meant, which Vorik had expected since all yenni were dim of the mind. Yet he could tell that the gentle way he'd spoken the words had calmed her fears a bit. Her eyes flicked down to his shaft, no doubt remembering the need of a meal, and he felt his man sac go nigh unto blue as it tightened further, ready to explode for her.

And then, oh, aye, and then, the alpha female gave herself up to the lure of a hot meal as her lips slowly clamped around the sensitive head of his manhood. Vorik groaned at the first touch, his muscles cording when he saw and felt her suctioning lips envelop the head in its entirety.

"Oh, aye," he moaned hoarsely, perspiration dotting his brow, wetting his shoulder-length black hair. His breathing grew labored as he watched her eyes close, as he heard her softly moan whilst she began attending to his cock. A rush of air came out from his lungs in a hiss as he gently guided her head up and down his shaft, his fingers twined through her hair as he pressed her closer to him.

She suckled him ferociously, getting more and more into the feeding as her eyes closed and she worked her suctioning lips vigorously up and down his staff. Her nipples hardened as she toyed with him, as she did what the females of her species had done since the advent of time to males of his species.

Vorik groaned when her small hands began massaging his man sac, gasping when he knew he was nigh close unto bursting already. Her ravenous tongue knew how to flick about his sensitive head; her nimble fingers knew just how much pressure to apply to his scrotum. He gasped again as he watched his cock disappear into the depths of her mouth, her eyes closed in bliss as she suckled up and down the length of him.

She took him in a frenzy, her suctioning mouth working faster and faster, the sound of lips meeting cock smacking throughout the nest. Vorik growled low in his throat, unable to stop his fangs from emerging from his gums. He cradled her head reverently at his groin, his silver eyes opening, then narrowing in crimson desire, as he watched her feast on him.

She suckled faster, then faster still, her silken amber head bobbing up and down upon his manhood. When her tiny hands began massaging his man sac in earnest in time with her sucks, his head fell back upon the animal hides and his muscles corded. She seemed to know 'twas time to make him spurt, for her suctioning mouth honed in on the sensitive head. She sucked upon it greedily whilst massaging his tight balls.

Oh, aye, Vorik thought, his mind nigh unto delirious. 'Twas bliss, this.

His entire body shuddered, then clenched hotly in anticipation of release. The yenni continued to work the magic of her kind upon him harder and harder still, her fingers massaging his scrotum whilst her lips pulled, sucked, and suctioned at the sensitive head.

"Zya," he roared.

Vorik exploded between her lips, his fangs jutting fully from his gums, whilst his entire body convulsed. She groaned as his seed spurted into her mouth, then closed her eyes as she fed from him, lapping up every last glowing drop of his silvery dew.

It was long minutes before he could catch his breath and even longer minutes before he could see again, for stars had exploded behind his eyes when he'd spurted and he had felt nigh close unto swooning from the intensity of his release. But at last, when finally he was able to steady himself and breathe normally again, he gazed down upon her lush form and his man sac instantly tightened for her.

Oh, aye, he thought headily, a smile of contentment pervading his lips as he nudged her face with gentle reverence back down toward his groin, this yenni was a hungry alpha without a doubt.

She studied him with an astonished expression for a few moments, her eyes clashing with his as she apparently decided what to do. But eventually, just as Vorik had thought she would—as he'd hoped she would—the beautiful, hungry she-beast latched her lips around the head of his manhood again and resumed the process of feeding from him.

Vorik lay back upon the muu animal hides with a dreamy sigh, his heavily muscled arms flung over his head in surrender to her appetite. He closed his eyes and smiled blissfully as her lips worked him up into a sexual frenzy, praying that 'twould take many sucklings before her belly felt full.

Verily, he thought on a gasp as his man sac tightened with seed, who needed a Bloodmate when a pet so fine as this one needed food.

Still, he was no saint, he knew. He enjoyed feeding her, but 'twould be bliss when she'd had her fill and he could stuff his cock into her wet, puffed up pussy.

Oh, aye. 'Twould be bliss.

Nancy wasn't sure if she'd gone insane or not, but four blowjobs later she decided that she had. Her jaw was so sore it was throbbing, yet every time the huge predator gazed down at her with stars in his eyes she'd find her lips latch-ing around his penis of seemingly their own accord and she'd begin the process of making him come all over again.

She sighed resignedly, realizing as she did that it was heady indeed to have a male gaze down at you as though you were a goddess. That the male doing the gazing was the most handsome and powerful man she'd ever laid eyes on only added to the giddiness. She knew he was young—he had to be young, regardless of his gigantic size. His reactions to her blowjobs were completely unschooled, and naively touching.

As he spurted the sweetest liquid she'd ever tasted between her lips for a mouth-shattering fifth time, she told herself that she had to be dreaming. He was eight feet tall, he had to weigh five hundred pounds or more, his eyes were silver when he was sated and crimson when he was angry or passionate, he had fangs, and he growled.

Definitely not what one would call a lucid reality.

And yet, weird as it was, she knew deep down inside that she wasn't dreaming. She knew that she was awake and that this gargantuan male would do all in his power to keep her from escaping him.

She felt a pang of fear course through her as she wondered what she could do to get away from him. He was handsome for sure, but handsome wasn't enough to keep her from wanting to go home.

But if she did find a way to escape while he was sleeping or otherwise unaware, what then? Nancy sighed as she laid down beside him, her head coming down to rest upon his chest, her mind too tired to reason out any escape attempts just now.

She had no idea where she was and no idea how to leave it behind. Where the witch had thrown her she could only guess.

Chapter 5

Vorik awoke in the silvery twilight with a tight man sac, the need to mate weighing down upon him mightily. He smiled as he cuddled his pet closer, the sound of her contented snoring causing him to chuckle.

Aye, she had fed well on him last moon-rising. Verily, she had suckled him nigh blind just as he'd hoped she would.

He sighed dreamily, his eyes still closed as his large hand ran down her lush backside to play with her tail whilst she slumbered. She was perfection, his pet. She was an exuberant suckler who would bring him many lifetimes of bliss. She was—

His brow furrowed as his hand fumbled about her backside. *Where was her tail?* he grumbled to himself. He felt no appendage at all there. Surely his pet had to have a tail! Where was—

"Ahh, gods."

Vorik's eyes flew open and darted downward, his silver gaze clashing with an intelligent brown one. His gaze narrowed as he looked at her, really looked at her, for the first time. Apparently his intense study of her features frightened her, for she swallowed nervously and looked away.

By the Ices of Shalor, he thought with surprise, the female was no yenni at all. She was humanoid—a humanoid wench.

Ahh, gods, what a dunce he was! He grimaced. Now that he viewed her in the harsh light of day, she had naught in common with a yenni other than creamy, pearly skin. She was too beautiful to be a yenni, and her eyes were too knowing.

But nay, Vorik silently qualified, he was not one known for being a lack-wit. He could have sworn she'd had a tail when first he'd ensnared her—aye she'd had a tail. Hadn't she?

Well, no matter, he grunted, his palm kneading the backside he refused to relinquish—humanoid or no. Whether she'd had a tail or his eyes had been playing tricks on him was irrelevant just now, for he knew with all certainty she had let loose the cry of an alpha female yenni desirous of a feeding. That much of last moon-rising's events was a certainty.

He grunted again, satisfied in his reasoning, contented in the knowledge that he was no dunce. Feeling amorous as his species was wont to do, he plucked the humanoid wench from her lying position and set her upon his lap so that her legs straddled him. She yelped a bit at first, her large breasts heaving up and down, and he figured correctly that she was frightened of his size.

Well, no matter. He would gentle her to his touch, then he would do the very deed he'd been nigh dying to do since he'd been a twelve-year-old pup.

Slowly, Vorik's dark head came up and his sharp, silver eyes clashed with her rich, dark ones. She swallowed nervously, looking away from him again, which was just as well, for his mouth had dropped open in shock.

By the tit of the she-god, his sins were worse than he'd thought!

Vorik groaned, sorely vexed with himself. His cheeks pinkened in embarrassment and shame as he considered the reality of what he'd done.

Not only was she no yenni, not only was she a humanoid, but she was something far more important and coveted than either of those things. She was the very elusive dream most males of his species spent lifetimes searching for and, sadly, many never found. She was his—all his—and no other's. And he'd found her on the very moon-rising he'd become a barbarian full grown.

"Oh, aye," he murmured as he felt his body respond to hers, as the need to mount her and impregnate her womb instinctually kicked in. Every cell in his body tingled as he drank in the scent of her. His manhood hardened with thoughts of gorging upon her blood and, oh aye, with tantalizing thoughts of her gorging upon his blood.

Vorik released a shaky breath as his hands clutched her hips and his fingers dug into the flesh there. He needed to mate her now, to sink himself deep inside of her and get a litter of pups on her the soonest.

She was his Bloodmate.

Nancy gasped when, in the blink of an eye, he reversed their positions and lowered his massive body between her comparatively small legs. She sighed, thinking it had taken being thrown into another world—most likely another planet entirely!—for her to feel small and delicate next to a man. A fanged man. A fanged man with a penis large enough to rend her into halves.

"*EEEK!*" Nancy pushed at the unmoving wall that was his chest, her legs flailing madly at either side of his hips. She hadn't been able to get even half of his shaft into her mouth last night—there was no way in the hell it was going between her legs.

"Forget it!" she fumed, her voice indignant. "The buck stops here, buddy."

For a woman who had been a spinster all of a day ago, this was just too much. Sucking on him was one thing—and she still wasn't certain what had possessed her to do that much!—but having him put it inside her was another thing altogether. She bet he'd never once suffered from a case of penis envy. No locker room ribbings for this guy.

Her hand slashed definitively through the air. "There is no way you will ever—*eek!*"

A growl of outrage erupted from his throat as fangs exploded through his gums. His once silver eyes turned crimson in anger, in lust, in possessiveness. He was anxious to get inside of her—very anxious, she knew, when he bent his head and nipped at her shoulder disapprovingly. She wondered if all the fighting in the world would keep him from sinking into her, which she feared could possibly kill her!

And yet, as anxious as she could tell he was to dominate her will and her body, he stilled himself atop her, waiting for . . . something. Waiting for her to calm herself, perhaps?

Nancy's lips pinched together in a frown as she considered the fact that his method was working. She *was* becoming calmer. And the moonstruck way that he was gazing down at her, the same worshipping, hopeful expression that King Kong had harbored as he'd watched Fay Wray's every movement, was doing its damnedest to work a number on her senses.

She sighed, her eyes closing and her hands coming up to rub at her temples. This was weirdness incarnate. The ultimate getting-kidnapped-by-a-mountain-man scenario. And what's worse, she had a perverse feeling that by the time all was said and done, she'd have become a willing captive.

Damn it!

Her nostrils flaring, Nancy's eyes flew open to meet her captor's and their gazes locked. He looked ferocious. Determined. His jaw was set, his fangs slightly bared, and his eyes were now pure crimson.

Oh damn, she thought as she began panting, she could feel him telepathically speaking into her mind. She had no idea what he was saying because she couldn't speak his tongue, but whatever the words were they were doing a number on her hormonally. She groaned as horniness the likes of which she'd never before felt lanced through her, then gasped as her womb began to contract.

She needed his flesh joined to hers, needed to feel him rocking in and out of her, needed him to impregnate her. She would obey him in all things, she thought unblinkingly, for she could do no other. She belonged to him forever. Verily, her body was but his vessel, ever ready to provide pleasure—

"Damn it!" she sniffed. Her eyes narrowed when she realized he'd been hypnotizing her. "Quit making me think things I don't want to think!"

He smiled slowly as an answer, then sent out a sensual mental wave that left her gaping like the village idiot.

Nancy closed her eyes and moaned, her body involuntarily writhing beneath the giant's. Good grief, she silently wailed, she was back to feeling like a dog in heat. Only this time the effect was a thousand times worse—and likely to drive her mad if he didn't enter her body soon.

"Please," she groaned, her breaths coming out in a series of short gasps.

To hell with worries about dying, she sniffed. She needed him inside her like she needed to breathe. She decided this was no time to contemplate how troublesome of a fact that was. She wrapped her legs around his waist without thinking about it, then reared up her hips and ground her soaking wet flesh against his groin.

He hissed.

"Please."

He settled himself comfortably between her legs, then bent his dark head to nip at her neck with his teeth. He punctured the skin there, causing a few droplets of her blood to trickle out onto his tongue. He lapped the beads of blood up, groaning as if she tasted like an elixir from the gods.

"Oh, lord," she groaned, her belly knotting with impending climax, "oh, yes." She felt delirious—good grief what was he doing to her?

She didn't know what instinct made her bite him, couldn't say what drove her to it, but in a frenzy of lust and intuition, Nancy's head shot up and she clamped down onto his jugular vein as hard as she could with her comparatively dull teeth. He began to writhe and moan, his low growl evolving into a fierce roar.

Incisors sliced cleanly into her jugular, causing her to

whimper from the human fear of death mingled with an evolving predator's ecstasy. She never let go of his jugular, though, and soon she would be glad she hadn't.

An orgasm exploded inside her as he drank her blood, the violence of it intense enough to make her body convulse. It didn't matter that Nancy's incisors were dull in comparison to the teeth of the male who was preparing to mount her. Her human teeth sank into his jugular as far as they could go, nicking him, causing him to bleed a single droplet of blood.

It was enough.

The moment the sweet taste of his blood hit her tongue, Nancy groaned as her body shook with yet another orgasm. She enjoyed the intensity so much that even when he made her release his neck so he could mount her the way he wanted to, she bit down onto his chest and drew blood, refusing to let go, moaning and groaning when orgasm after orgasm rocked through her.

"Oh, aye, little one," he said hoarsely.

Her body stilled. Her teeth fell away from his chest as reality set in. She was drinking a man's blood.

"Oh, God," she dramatically wailed.

"I need to mount you, *vorah*," the giant said thickly, seemingly unaware of her tumultuous thoughts.

His silver eyes glazed over as he nudged her down to lie fully upon her back. He settled himself on his knees between her legs, clutching her hips with his hands and spreading her thighs wide.

"Wh–what are y–you doing?"

What a dumb question!

"Mounting you," he said in a hoarse voice.

Against her volition, Nancy's nipples hardened and elongated as she watched the gargantuan-sized predator prepare to thrust inside her for the first time. Eyes closed and nostrils flaring, she could tell by the look of impending nirvana smothering his features that the eight-foot giant getting ready to mate her had never been with another woman. Never.

A five-hundred-pound virgin.

A five-hundred-pound virgin who drinks blood and possesses a penis the size of a small whale.

Ooookay.

"Oh, dear," Nancy whimpered, her logical mind at war with her eyes—eyes that were busy drinking in the intoxicating sight of his heavily muscled body. Why did her body react to him as if it had been pre-programmed to? "P–Perhaps we should start slower," she hedged, glancing uneasily up at his fangs. "Maybe holding hands would be nice—"

She said no more when he looked at her as though she'd gone mad. Good lord, she probably had gone mad! That certainly explained this new world she was inhabiting. Perhaps she and the other mental wards at the local asylum were visiting here at the same time. Right after they'd had tea with Napoleon. Nervously, her hand darted up to push the spectacles she always wore up the bridge of her nose. Oh that's right. She wasn't wearing any spectacles.

Damn it!

Nancy closed her eyes and groaned, a melodramatic feeling of martyrdom overtaking her. What was so wrong with being a spinster? Why had she ever thought to get a new life?

" 'Twill be all right, little one," he murmured. "Verily, I could never hurt you."

Her eyes flew open. For the first time it dawned on her that she could understand what he was saying. And, she thought bewilderedly, he wasn't speaking English by any stretch of the imagination. "H–How . . ."

"Thy blood is in me." He bent his head and sipped at her neck again, causing her to gasp. "And mine in you," he murmured.

His gaze narrowed, eyelids heavy. He grabbed his thick penis by the root, placing the head near her hole. His jaw clenched.

"Vorah."

Nancy gasped as he impaled her, seating himself to the hilt. He groaned as he ground his cock into her, his jugular vein bulging.

It hadn't killed her after all.

"Oh, my," she breathed out, her back arching.

"Vorah," he ground out, sweat dotting his brow, "I've the need to impregnate you, little one."

Vorah—Bloodmate.

The human equivalent to *wife*.

Oh, lord.

Nancy gazed up at the gigantic male whose flesh had fully penetrated hers and was surprised by the array of emotions she felt just looking at him. It worried her really, for it meant that not only had her body been pre-programmed to need him, but her heart had been as well. But pre-programmed by whom? By what? She sighed, very confused.

Vorik stroked into her flesh slowly, the look of rapture on his face heady enough to tug at Nancy's heartstrings. She closed her eyes briefly, opening them on a sigh, the poignant feeling of being his first lover doing a tap dance on her emotions, and her libido. She actually found herself wishing that she knew what to call him.

Vorik, he answered in her mind. *Thy Bloodmate.*

Their eyes met. Nancy nibbled at her lower lip as her reticence dissolved.

"I'm Nancy," she whispered.

Vorik slid in and out of her, groaning as he slowly mounted her. "Nawncy," he ground out. He held her thighs apart with his large hands, his hips rotating in between them as he thrust into her flesh.

She gasped, her nipples hardening.

Vorik bent his head to her chest, his tongue darting out to curl around one jutting nipple. Nancy moaned loudly. His tongue was rough like a cat's, the gentle sandpaper sensation sending tremors zinging through her. He sucked on her nipple for a long time while he slowly thrust into her. Wet and aroused, she could hear her pussy making sucking sounds with each of his outstrokes.

He flicked at her nipple with his tongue, then raised his dark head. "Are you ready for more, beautiful one?" Vorik murmured.

"Yes," she gasped, her hips arching up to meet his thrusts.

He closed his eyes and picked up the pace, pumping into her flesh in deep, wild strokes, moaning and groaning the entire time. Sweat broke out onto his forehead. The muscles in his arms clenched and corded. His teeth gritted as he rode her into oblivion, never wanting the sensations to end.

Nancy watched his face the entire time, gasping as he took her. It was a heady feeling, owning the first pussy a man ever fucked. The expression on his face was indescribable in its intensity. He looked delirious with pleasure, yet she could tell from the way his jaw was clenched as he rocked in and out of her that he was doing his damnedest to keep from reaching orgasm. He wanted the euphoria to last. He never wanted to stop mounting her.

She moaned when he rode her harder, his hips pistoning faster and faster between her thighs. She could hear her flesh sucking him in, trying to hold on to his cock every time he rocked back and forth.

"Aye," she heard him growl.

His eyes were closed, as if concentrating intently on the feel of her cunt. Vorik mounted her mercilessly, holding back nothing. He took her harder and faster, deeper and more ferociously. Over and over, again and again.

Nancy gasped as incisors sliced cleanly into her neck.

She came instantly, screaming as she threw her hips back at him, meeting his every possessive thrust.

Vorik gorged on his Bloodmate with a growl, feeding on her blood as he stuffed his stiff cock inside of her. He moaned and groaned throughout every last orgasm, allowing her as much pleasure as he could, taking from her as much pleasure as he could.

He wouldn't be able to touch her whilst she incubated so he wanted the moment to last forever, but knew that soon the deed would be fully done.

When she came again, writhing and moaning, throwing her hips at him like a wanton, he could take no more torture. She wasn't of his breed and mayhap wouldn't know that it was time to be one with him. He raised a finger to his neck, a single fingernail spiking up. Nostrils flaring, he nicked open his jugular and lowered it to her.

She drank of him, became one with him, never thought to deny him. He roared at the euphoric sensations swamping him, the feeling akin to never-ending orgasmic release. She was his now; he had branded her.

Only when Vorik knew the deed was done, when he was certain she'd drank enough of him to evolve, did he allow himself the final, harsh release. Realizing as he did that he would not get to make love to her for a sennight, he glutted on her blood and cunt as long as 'twas possible, hedonistically enjoying every sip, every thrust.

"Vorah."

He came on a loud roar, his eyes crimson with passion, with possession. The orgasm went on and on and on, 'til finally his man sac had been emptied of all seed.

When it was over, when both of their breathing returned to normal, Vorik smiled down at her, his expression worshipful.

"Many thanks, little one," he murmured. " 'Twas more bliss than I can say."

Nancy grinned. "You weren't too bad your—"

Her eyes rounded. She gasped as she felt her breath slowly leave her body.

"Vorik," she panted, "what the . . ."

"You are evolving, my love." Vorik disentangled his body from Nancy's so as not to impede the process. He smiled. " 'Twill be but one sennight in the cocoon."

Oooookay. So maybe she'd let things go just a bit too far.

I know you didn't just say what I think you just said!

Aye, my love, I did.

You've got to be joking! And stop talking into my mind! Arrrg!

"A c–cocoon?" Nancy cried out. Gasping for air, she rolled onto her side, noticing for the first time that a web was forming around her hands—a thick web of sticky material. *"Oh my God!"*

She screamed, trying to bat the web away with her hands, but it was growing and thickening, and climbing up her arms. "Help me!" she screamed, jumping up to her feet. She gasped as more air left her lungs, then she fell to her knees.

Calm thyself, vorah.

No!

She could have sworn she heard him grunt in her mind.

Nancy watched in dawning horror as the web made its way up her arms and began encasing her fully, all the way down to her toes. Unable to scream from a lack of oxygen in her lungs, she cried out mentally, rolling her body to the far side of the nest.

Vorik came after her, apparently not wanting her to harm her cocoon. *"Vorah!"* he commanded her. "Calm thyself and quit moving anon!"

But Nancy was delirious, wild, frantic. She rolled farther, and Vorik stepped closer. The nest teetered and swayed.

"Vorah!"

Cold terror knifed through her as the nest collapsed and she began plummeting toward the ground at bloodcurdling speed. She bypassed winged animals, mountain peaks, and—oh God—a mountain base, as she plummeted down, down, down, down . . .

She was almost completely encased, nothing but her eyes showing as the cocoon turned over so Nancy could see up instead of down.

Vorik.

He was coming after her, swooping down from the heavens.

But he was no longer a man.

Silver body. Silver wings. Fangs. Crimson eyes.

Nancy silently screamed as the cocoon encased her fully, her last conscious thought before her breath entirely left her that the man she'd just made love to was a gargoyle.

And worse yet, he had turned her into one, too.

Vorik swooped down and caught the vorah-sac in his arms, careful not to snag it with his teeth as was the automatic instinct possessed by his kind when in kor-tar form. But then usually when one was descending upon a body 'twas as a predator seizing prey so he cared not whether his fangs ripped through the animal's flesh. Since this was the cocoon of his evolving Bloodmate, however, he cared mightily.

He cradled the vorah-sac in his arms, cautious of her delicate state at all times. She was defenseless just now, unable to protect herself whilst she incubated, and so 'twas her Bloodmate she depended upon at this time for safety more so than she ever would again.

When Nancy awoke, he knew the metabolic changes within would cause her to be as deadly as was he—mayhap even more so—for he'd never heard tell of a species of predators in any dimension where the female wasn't deadlier than the male. Mayhap 'twas to compensate for the fact that she would be much smaller than a lot of the species of prey they would stalk together throughout their seven lifetimes.

There were many characteristics that the barbarians of Khan-Gor shared with other predators, the most fundamental one the difference between the genders. Although Nancy would be gifted with the ability to kill attackers and seize prey in many deadly ways that Vorik could not, she would never be able to best her own Bloodmate—never.

Vorik smiled at that thought, thinking the gods showed much in the way of smarts. Verily, if the deadly female was able to bring down the male she had mated with, then males would be killed off left and right, mayhap every time their vorahs got into a temper. Since Bloodmates mated for life, 'twould be foolhardy of nature to allow for such, for the predator populace would die out and those lower on the foodchain would become too great in numbers.

And so it had come to pass through the long process of evolution that the Khan-Gori male was possessed of two gifts the female was not: whilst in animal form his silver skin was impenetrable from puncture wounds dealt by a Bloodmate, and whilst in either form he could mesmerize his Bloodmate should he so desire it. Those two attributes, working in conjunction with his larger, fiercer size, gave the Khan-Gori male eternal dominion over his deadly wife.

Vorik dismissed his stray thoughts as he scanned the grounds and mountain passes for a safe place to make camp 'til the sennight of incubation had passed and his Bloodmate emerged from her cocoon. He couldn't chance flying all the way back to F'al Vader lands this way with her in his arms, for if a rival predator made battle with him, he would be forced to choose between dropping the vorah-sac to fight, which would kill Nancy in the process, or allowing himself to be killed by a male from another pack. Since Vorik would choose to die with his Bloodmate rather than drop her, he knew 'twould mean death to them both.

His crimson eyes located an empty cavern below that his visual acuity told him was not currently being inhabited. He swooped down to make haste toward it, realizing as he did from years' worth of hunting that the cavern was nestled within neutral lands unclaimed by any pack. 'Twould do.

Vorik snarled, a warning to weaker lifeforms below that did they wish to see the next morn, they would clear out the cavern immediately and stay gone until he and his Bloodmate left it behind. His acute hearing picked up the vibrations of scampering feet and, verily, by the time he arrived with his vorah-sac and had shape-shifted to humanoid form, all signs of life were long gone.

Vorik carried Nancy into the ice-coated cavern, his Bloodmate securely cradled in his arms. After a week of unwavering diligence, he could return to his pack, his vorah in tow.

Chapter 6

One week later

Nancy's breath came back in a rush, her lungs heaving and expelling a huge gush of air. Crimson eyes flew open and fangs exploded from her gums as she instinctively sought out her Bloodmate. In a behavior pattern that had genetically been programmed into her during the incubation period, she exploded from the cocoon with a fierce roar, able to do so by a lining of deadly spikes that jutted out of the skin cells on her forearms.

Unable to think of anything save the need for Vorik's nearness, and voraciously aroused after having not mated during the entire week she'd been cocooned, Nancy flew at top speed out of the cavern, her heightened sense of smell detecting that Vorik was a mile off, somewhere in the vicinity of the mouth of the icy riverbed below.

The scent of him aroused her further, inducing her nipples to harden and her belly to knot in anticipation of being mounted. The moment her Bloodmate saw her descending upon him, his lips formed a snarl as he shape-shifted into kor-tar form and took flight toward her.

Their silver bodies came together in a midair clash, and Vorik immediately sank his teeth into her neck. Nancy gasped at the arousal, her need to be impregnated by the large male too instinctual to resist him. That he now looked like a gargoyle, that he was fanged and winged and his eyes were crimson—all of these things her earthly memory cells were wary of, but the need to be impregnated was too pressing to pay them much heed.

As her Bloodmate lowered them to the ground with a fierce growl, then forced her bodily onto her hands and knees, she could think of nothing—*nothing*—but being fucked. It was as if she'd never been human, as if her body harbored no memories of an existence before she'd emerged from the cocoon.

Vorik entered her from behind on a dangerous growl, his thick, swollen penis impaling her warm flesh in one thrust. She hissed at his roughness, glancing over her shoulder to snarl at him. He growled in response, then nipped at her shoulder with his teeth to show her who was in control. He pounded into her cunt from behind and she yipped in response, whimpering like a puppy that'd had her tail stepped on at the chastisement.

Vorik immediately soothed her, his tongue darting out to lap at her shoulder while he kept up his steady tempo of thrusts. Nancy gasped in pleasure, then began to mate with him, throwing her hips back at him to increase the friction and the deepness.

Aye, little one, she heard a hoarse voice in her mind say. *I've missed thy presence sorely. Fuck me with that sweet cunt.*

She did as he bade her, throwing her flesh back at him, moaning and groaning as he pounded into her body, hissing with ecstasy as his sharp fingernails dug into the flesh of her hips. She didn't understand why the sensation of his fingernails piercing her skin felt so good, only knew that it did. It was like a sensual massage, akin to the way it would feel if her clitoris was being rubbed.

His tight balls slapped against her flesh while he possessively slammed in and out her. Nancy burst on a growl, her wet flesh contracting as she came.

The orgasm was a thousand times stronger than anything she'd experienced as a human. She moaned and groaned, writhed and twisted, as Vorik continued to impale her over and over, again and again.

Nancy wanted him to come. Her womb contracted with feverish desperation.

Vorik . . .

She could sense he was coming. Every egg in her uterus tingled.

I wish it to last, he mentally bellowed. His teeth gritted. *I wish it to—ahh, gods.*

* * *

Vorik exploded on a reverberating roar, the feeling of her pussy contracting around his cock forcing him into it. He had heard tell that a Bloodmate's cunt could suck a Khan-Gori male's staff dry, but not until now did he know that the gossip was true.

Verily, her flesh squeezed him in a series of intense contractions until he could withstand no more, until he was roaring and growling from the pleasure of it. Vorik pounded into her wet flesh twice more, then clawed her hips to force her into peaking with him as he emptied his seed deep inside her.

They fucked for three more hours. Vorik became more animalistic with each mating, drinking her blood to heighten the delirious ecstasy, scratching at her hips to make her tremor and convulse around his cock.

He took her with the violence of his species, primal in a way he could never be whilst she was in her humanoid form. Only one time during the entire mating did she snarl at him to get off her, and that was only after she'd been effectually impregnated with a pup and wanted some rest. Vorik, a virgin just a week ago, wanted more and more and more of her pussy, refusing to stop until he burst again and again inside her.

When Nancy protested with a growl, his answering roar of denial followed by a sharp nick to the shoulder silenced her. Obediently, she pressed one side of her face to the ground and hoisted her hips up further that he might root in her as deeply and as much as he desired.

Vorik grunted in satisfaction, a snort of male arrogance puncturing the night as he impaled her flesh over and over again with his. Amidst a mating frenzy, he pummeled her roughly, mounting her for another solid hour, spurting seed into her flesh more times than either of them could count.

When finally he was sated, when his balls were drained of all seed, Vorik curled his gargantuan-sized body around hers, and they prepared to sleep together that way, still in kor-tar form so that the icy elements around them had no negative effect.

Nancy grunted, wanting closer contact.

Vorik slid his penis into her from behind, that both of them had the constant contact they craved.

They fell asleep, two Bloodmates bound together in every way possible.

Chapter 7

Nancy awoke the next morning in humanoid form. Vorik's body, still in kor-tar form, was curled around her, thwarting the icy chill of the landscape from adversely affecting her. Without his skin emitting constant, toasty-warm heat, she guessed she'd be dead in the matter of an hour. She shivered at the thought, then snuggled up closer to him as a matter of self-preservation.

Nancy worried her bottom lip as she realized for the first time that Vorik was still in his gargoyle form. She'd seen him that way last night, but last night she had looked at him through the eyes of a similar predator. This morning, right now, she found herself afraid to get her first good look at him through a human's eyes, for when she did she would know precisely what it was she had evolved into.

Her memories of the metabolic changes she'd undergone while cocooning weren't numerous. And those that did exist weren't so much memories as they were impressions. A feeling of rebirth, of rejuvenation, of acquiring heightened senses, and of gaining more acute—everything. Eyes that had once required spectacles or contact lenses to see could now scan terrain a mile or more off in the distance. Ears that she'd once considered to be superiorly adept at hearing would now feel deaf in comparison if she were to listen through them again.

Nancy closed her eyes briefly, drawing in a calming breath of air. She needed to see him, she told herself. She needed to know what it was human eyes would see when they looked at him—and when they looked at her. How could she ever hope to go back to Earth if—

Dear God, she thought on a pang of emotion, why was the thought of leaving Vorik, a man she'd known all of a week, so horrible? So empty?

She sighed, for the first time sincerely doubting she'd be able to feel sane without him in her life. Not just in her life, but in her constant presence. The reassuring, steady beat of his heart thumping gently against her back did more to quell her restlessness than she wished it did. Because that quelling, that calming, could only mean one thing: she well and truly would go insane without having him near her.

Nancy's head came up slowly, her round brown eyes finding Vorik's alert crimson red ones. He was awake. Awake and in gargoyle form. Her breath caught. They stared into each other's eyes.

In that instant, as she witnessed the sadness in his gaze, as she heard a low, pained sound rumble gently up from his throat, she knew what Vorik was thinking without needing him to mentally or verbally send the words out to her. He was hurting on the inside, wondering to himself if she'd ever be able to truly love a man who was also a beast.

In a rush of impressions she saw the planet Khan-Gor's past swim before her mind's eye, a past that included the closing off of the silver-ice planet to outsiders. A fear of their people, namely what their people were able to do genetically, had caused males from other planets to seek them out in an effort to destroy their race.

In a way, it had worked.

For several millenniums the planet had remained shielded in an invisible cloak of ice until all outsiders had forgotten of their existence and the pack leaders felt it was safe to lower their guard a bit. Even then no Khan-Goris had ventured off planet until the situation had become so grim that the males of their species were left with little choice but to look elsewhere for their Bloodmates, for they weren't likely to find them on Khan-Gor.

Indeed, Nancy saw as she closed her eyes, female-born Khan-Goris were all but nonexistent, their numbers sparse. Nature, it seemed, had never intended for Khan-Gori males to mate within their own race, a phenomenon that no doubt kept the gene pools aired out and healthy, and kept females who were transformed into predators breeding dominant, robust sons. To breed within the race could cause madness amongst the offspring, and in one fatal case it had created a monster.

She opened her mind further to Vorik and saw a scene replaying in his memories. The memory was of Vorik's father imparting unto his son the telling of a legend, of how he had been the first Khan-Gori male in three thousand years to venture off planet in search of his Bloodmate, how he had found Jana, Vorik's mother, and how he had brought her home.

But nothing, of course, had been quite that simple.

Nancy's heart clenched when she saw Vorik's first memory, a memory that had occurred just moments after his birth. His mother, Jana, who had been on the run from Vorik's father at the time, had been frightened of her kor-tar son upon seeing him flutter out from between her legs. So frightened, in fact, that she had refused to hold him in her arms or to feed him at her breast after she had birthed him.

Nancy's bottom lip trembled as the scene continued to play out.

Jana, who had refused to shape-shift into her kor-tari form beyond her first emergence from the cocoon, had spent the next few days staring off into space unblinking, a blank expression on her face. Vorik had cried often from within their hiding place, the cries of a newborn baby needing food. But she had ignored him, hearing nothing, seeing nothing, never acknowledging his existence.

And then one day, thankfully before Vorik had starved to death, his mother had regained her broken mind. Jana had been out of the cave they were hiding in, wandering about aimlessly, when a deadly intruder had snuck in with the intent of killing her tiny son.

His mother, who had been weakened at the time from days of not eating, had sensed the intrusion into the cavern and, in a burst of power and speed, had shape-shifted into her gargoyle form and killed the intruder with one swift backhanded slap. Because of the spikes that jut out from a female's arms when in animal form, the kill had been quick and efficient, impaling the enemy and killing him instantaneously.

When it was finally over and Jana knew that the threat to her son had passed, she had broken down crying, regaining her sanity in the process. *Forgive me, Vorik,* she had sobbed, at last placing the helpless newborn at her breast. *For the love of the goddess, please forgive me, my son.*

Nancy's eyes opened slowly, unshed tears causing her lashes to glisten as her gaze clashed with her Bloodmate's. Vorik had, of course, forgiven his mother, for he loved her fiercely. But his heart had never forgotten the rejection.

Vorik made no movement to force Nancy to stay close to him. He simply lay there and waited for her judgment, his sad crimson eyes flicking over her face. *Can you love me?* she thought she heard him say softly in her mind. *Can you accept me for what I am?*

Nancy's breath caught as she looked at him through the eyes of a humanoid, as she studied his features and found her hand coming up to gently memorize his face with her palm and fingers. His eyes closed briefly at the soothing contact, opening again to watch her expression, to see for himself how she felt.

In that poignant moment, all thoughts of earth, all memories of her former life and friends, dimmed in importance until they had all but faded away. Nancy smiled softly at her Bloodmate, finding nothing lacking, realizing as she did that he was the most powerful and glorious life-form she'd ever been granted the privilege of seeing.

He was carved of sleek silver, his muscles plentiful and fierce. His face, even in kor-tar form, was harshly handsome. Though he was bald like any gargoyle would be while in this form, she found the effect made him appear all the more formidable and virile, not to mention terribly sexy.

"Yes," she murmured, her eyes meeting his. She smiled, searching his face. "I can love you."

His breathing hitched as he stared at her, but he spoke not a word. And then, in the blink of an eye, he picked her up in his arms and flew off at top speed, neither descending nor slowing until they reached the cavern she'd incubated in while evolving in the cocoon.

He laid her down gently on a bed of animal hides, then came down on his knees before her, still in kor-tar form. Nancy experienced a moment's panic when he splayed her thighs wide before him, then bent his head and licked from her anus to her clit in one wet, rough swipe. She remembered how violently they'd mated as gargoyles the evening prior, so she felt a slight hesitation as it became apparent that he wanted to mount her while she was still in human form.

Their gazes locked. "I shall never hurt you, little one," he said softly. He took a calming breath. "Please do this thing for me, that I might know in my heart you accept me as both man and beast."

Nancy smiled, unafraid. She knew he'd never hurt her. She'd only needed the reassurance. "Okay," she whispered back in his language.

His breath rushed out as he lowered his face between her legs and lapped at her pussy with his rough tongue. She gasped immediately, for his tongue in kor-tar form was even more abrasive than it was in humanoid form, which sent tremors immediately jolting through her. When she considered the sinfully provocative sight they made, a human woman who was willingly spreading her legs for a gargoyle's wicked sexual ministrations, her nipples hardened into painfully tight peaks.

Nancy glanced down to where his mouth was lapping at her flesh and shivered with arousal. His silver gargoyle face was pressed against her pussy, his crimson eyes watching her as he suckled her clit. He built her to a peak in a matter of moments, the sucks he made to her clit so fast that it looked as though he was munching on her flesh. She groaned, her head falling back against the animal hides, her eyes closing as her nipples jutted up in arousal.

"Vorik."

He sucked on her clit harder, his rough tongue simultaneously flicking the sensitive head in a show of sensual accomplishment no human male could ever master. She bucked up on a groan, then wrapped her legs around his neck and pressed his face in closer to her pussy.

Vorik growled against her clit, vibrating it even as he sucked and flicked at it. Nancy screamed in pleasure, gasping out his name as her entire body convulsed on a loud moan of completion. Blood rushed to her face, heating it. Blood rushed to her nipples, elongating them.

Vorik raised his head from her soaked flesh, then curled his rough tongue around one jutting nipple, soothing it while further arousing it. She sighed contentedly, her eyes still closed as she stroked his gargoyle head.

And then, oh, lord, and then, Vorik raised his silver head from her breast, licked her nipple one more time, and settled his huge silver body so that he sat on his knees between her legs. He lifted her hips, his fingernails scoring them.

"Oh, yes." Nancy's breathing grew choppier, her nipples harder, as she watched the sinful display of a gargoyle—a male many humans would call a demon—mount her pale white body, the body of a human woman.

His crimson eyes met her wide brown ones. His lips

parted in a slight snarl, baring his fangs. She licked her lips, recognizing it as a gesture of arousal on his part. She moaned when his fingernails raked her hips again before his large hands reached her thighs and spread them apart.

On a growl he entered her, seating himself fully, his crimson eyes narrowed into slits of desire. Nancy groaned as she watched his silver cock invade her human body, the sight of her wet pussy sucking him into her flesh an erotic one.

"Vorik," she breathed out, reaching up and running one finger along his left incisor. He shivered in reaction. "Feed from me," she murmured.

His scarlet eyes widened, not having expected her to accept that part of their mating so soon, so fully.

He growled as his fangs pierced the tender flesh of her neck, his hips rocking back and forth to pound inside of her as he drank of her blood. Nancy came violently, instantly, her moans and groans echoing throughout the cavern as he feasted at her neck, as her body quivered and convulsed from the fierce contractions.

"Vorik."

His gargoyle head raised from her neck, their gazes clashing as he concentrated on mounting her. She saw his teeth grit as he staved off his orgasm, knowing as she did that he wanted a longer mating before he came.

From somewhere deep inside himself he must have found his control, for Nancy's breath caught as she watched through human eyes while her Bloodmate took her in his beast form. He went wild, primal, his fangs baring fully as he sank his cock into her over and over, again and again.

She screamed from the pleasure, knowing every orgasm erupting from within was as much from watching a gargoyle fuck her as from the fucking itself.

Vorik rotated his hips and slammed into her, his fingernails grazing gently at her hips. His low growl lasted the entire time, throughout every one of her orgasms, throughout the entire mating ritual.

When he could stand no more, when he thought he'd go insane if he didn't come, he pounded into her one last time, then on a dominant roar, spurt his hot cum deep inside her.

Minutes later when the urgency had passed, Nancy found herself once again snuggling up against her Bloodmate to sleep. Only this time it wasn't the body of a female predator seeking the warmth and security of the beast. It was the body of a humanoid woman.

Chapter 8

One week later

Nancy awoke first, standing up after slowly disentangling their bodies. Last night she had played Fay Wray to his King Kong again, wanting him to take her in his kor-tar form rather than in his humanoid form. She had thoroughly enjoyed every wicked moment of it.

She wasn't certain why, really. She couldn't explain what it was that caused her to feel so aroused by something so simple as her Bloodmate mating her while he was shape-shifted.

Making love with a gargoyle, she thought on a grin, had a lot to recommend it.

Nancy blew out a resigned breath, smiling to herself. She more than loved Vorik. She was *in* love with him as well.

Hadn't the tiniest part of her, as unrealistic as she'd always known it was, secretly wished Fay Wray would fall as in love with King Kong as the giant ape had with his tiny human captive every time the old black and white movie had been shown on TV? But the real Fay Wray never had, for every time the movie played, she was as frantic to escape King Kong as she'd been the last time. And an hour later, the beloved beast would be dead, having fallen from atop the Empire State Building in his desperation to recapture the tiny woman he loved.

Nancy's eyes closed sadly as the truth hit her. If she ever ran from Vorik, the same fate would befall him. He'd do anything, including give up his life, just to be able to hold her in his arms. The thought of another male anywhere near her would kill him in a fundamental way no human mind could truly grasp. But because of their blood bond, because of the fact her genetics had been altered, she was able to understand.

She *did* understand. And because she did, she knew she would never leave him. Not that she had planned to anyway. As frightening as this new world was, Khan-Gor was now her home and Vorik was her mate. As terrified as she was to face what the future held, she realized with gut instinct that the future most definitely did not hold Earth.

Besides, she thought with a harrumph, she had fangs now. Fangs and wings. She could turn into a gargoyle. And she had orgasms every time she drank blood.

Good grief! As if she could go back home! She'd either be locked up in a mental ward or studied in some weirdo's lab for the remainder of her days.

Nancy's eyes flicked over to where Vorik slept, his humanoid body relaxed in deep slumber. She smiled. Her gentle giant. He looked so innocent while sleeping, even though she knew that when awake he was as fierce as a raptor.

She studied him a moment longer, then glanced away from her mate, her mind fast-forwarding to later on in the day when they would arrive on F'al Vader lands. They had taken their time getting here, wanting to further explore each other's minds and bodies before Vorik took her back to his lair.

Maybe, just maybe, Nancy told herself, joining his pack wouldn't be as frightening as she'd been telling herself it would be. She knew, after all, that Vorik would never hurt her. Nor would he allow another to do so.

He loved her—he was in love with her. The last week they'd spent together, making love and hunting, talking about nothing and everything, laughing together—all of it had only further solidified their special bond. And the lovemaking. Oooh, the lovemaking!

As her hourly need came upon her, Nancy allowed her form to shimmer and transform into her other, kor-tari self. She grinned, her fangs exploding from her gumline as she did so.

She heard her mate awaken from behind her, roused by the scent of her arousal. His lips formed a snarl as he bared his fangs and shape-shifted, growling as he exploded in the air toward her, their bodies clashing.

Nancy hadn't mated Vorik while in kor-tari form since

the evening she'd emerged from her cocoon. She hissed when his sharp nails dug into her flesh, deciding to immediately remedy that oversight.

To hell with going back to Earth. Her eyebrows wriggled. Nancy was home at last.

Epilogue

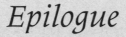

Ten Yessat years later

Nancy F'al Vader, nee Nancy Lombardo, grinned down at the tiny newborn pup feeding at her breast. She'd delivered five litters in ten years' time, though her first and last birthings had produced only one son apiece. Thank God.

Nancy still grimaced when she remembered the long, painful ordeal of the fourth birthing two years past. She had delivered five sons in that litter. Five! By the time the runt had made his way into the world, his tiny gargoyle body emerging from between her legs and taking flight, Nancy had begun to feel like a vending machine.

She smiled at the memory, recalling the way her tiny son had flown into her arms the minute he saw her, snuggling against her body and sighing contentedly. The same as another son, her youngest son, was doing now.

"He is perfect," Vorik murmured, his silver eyes finding

his Bloodmate's dark ones. He glanced back down at tiny Xorak and gently ran a finger over the small kor-tar head. "Just like his mother."

Nancy snorted at that. "You're just trying to get in my good graces," she teased. "So I don't throw you out of bed again."

He grunted at the recent memory, not having a care for it. "Can I help it if I go off into snoring fits after you've sated me in the bedfurs?" His eyes narrowed, flicking from silver to crimson. "Verily, 'tis a crime and a travesty to deny me thy body, vorah." His hand slashed definitively through the air. "I will never allow thus again, whether or not it causes me to snore."

She harrumphed, reveling in the debate. She couldn't help it. The lawyer in her, she supposed. "You gargoyles are all alike," she goaded him. "If ya can't take the lovin', stay out of the oven."

Vorik bent his dark head and nipped her on the shoulder, eliciting a yip. And a shiver. When his face reemerged into her line of vision, his expression was solemn. "Jesting aside, little one, I thank you for yet another beautiful son." He kissed the tip of her nose, then smiled. "I love you, Nancy," he murmured.

He pronounced her name *Nawncy*—it always made her smile. She ran her hand gently over his jaw. "I love you too, Vorik."

Later that evening, when all the pups were abed, Vorik joined her in their bedfurs with a wolf-eating grin on his face, a dimple popping out on either cheek. "Shall we play the yenni game anon, little one?"

Nancy ran her tongue seductively across her lower lip. She knew how much Vorik loved the yenni game. She would pretend to be a starving, voracious alpha yenni at market, while her Bloodmate played the role of the horny virgin trader desperate to feed her. Not too far off base from how they'd originally found each other, she thought bemusedly.

She wiggled her eyebrows at him. "I think that old sword is around here somewhere. You remember my sword? The one you mistook for a yenni tail ten Yessat years ago?"

Vorik chuckled at the memory. "Aye."

Nancy smiled at her Bloodmate, vastly contented. With him. With their sons. With herself. With life.

She was glad she hadn't taken that job in Alaska. Very glad indeed.

" *'Twill be a long journey,*" the old witch murmured. Her palm came up and rested on Nancy's forehead as she continued to study her face. *"But 'twill be worth the sacrifices when all is said and done. And love shall be yers."*

The old witch had been right. Love was most definitely hers. And, damn, was it beautiful.

And that, Nancy thought, her smile turning into laughter as Vorik assumed his virgin-trader-at-the-bartering-stalls role, was enough said.